Letters from Emily

M.L. Pennock

Cover design by 315 Designs

For Mom

The strongest woman I know.

Table of Contents

Chapter 1

Emily

"Bride's side or groom's?" he asks, holding his arm out for me as I step into the church.

"Uh ... bride. And you are?" I question. Having not met some of the groomsmen is leaving me a bit vulnerable. My voice has a hoarseness to it that draws a curious look from him. I can hear it and I don't think it quite fits my face or body. To my own ears it even has some sexy and unique quality to it, and I feel the heat rise in my cheeks.

"Brian Stratford. Friend of the groom and usher," he says as I wrap my arm around his elbow. He slowly begins walking me down the aisle. It's difficult to think straight, considering I should be doing this myself in a few weeks. "I'm at your service ..."

He stops with me beside a pew, waiting for me to respond before taking my seat. I could lie and not give him my real name. There are enough people here that I can get lost in the crowd after the service. Lies aren't what tumble from my lips as his blue eyes sparkle and a dimple appears in his right cheek.

"Emily. Emily Long. Since you're in the wedding, I assume you'll be at the reception. Can I also assume you'll save me a dance?" I don't want him to say no. It's been lonely the last few weeks and I would like to follow through with my plan to have as much fun tonight as I can.

"Well, Emily, I think that can be arranged." He smiles again as I take my seat, pushes his hands into his tuxedo pants pockets, and retreats to the back of the church.

~*~*~*~

Shana always wanted her wedding to be small. She got just that when she chose to say her "I do" in the white clapboard church she grew up attending. I think, in all, there were a hundred guests, but the size of the sanctuary couldn't contain the joy spilling over between Shana and Gavin.

The reception site is a different story. The large converted carriage barn can easily hold three times as many people between the indoor ballroom, bar area, and bed and breakfast upstairs, and there certainly are more people who have come to the party than bothered to attend the nuptials.

"Still saving that dance for me?" I hear softly behind me just above the music drifting in from the other room.

I escaped the reception when Gavin and Shana went to cut the cake. It's been a pleasure having time alone with my thoughts and my Cosmopolitan. The bartender was keeping his distance, and I didn't see him look up from his phone until Brian walked up and leaned on the bar beside me. It likely could have been my imagination, but the bartender's face seemed to fall a bit when Brian entered my personal space. It could be I want to feel wanted again, even if for a moment that wanting is by a man in a bowtie taking shit from drunk wedding guests. I'm craving the feeling of being needed.

"I thought you were supposed to be the one saving dances for me?" I tip my head to the side so I can see him. Twisting a straw between my fingers, I wonder if this is what flirting feels like as an adult. I haven't done this in years. I didn't think I would ever have to do this again, actually. Not until Adam told me he wasn't ready to be tied. It was the same night he told me to keep the ring he bought. "You've been busy two-stepping with the bride's sister. I figured you forgot about me."

"You're pretty unforgettable and I really like this song. I mean, very few men can sing love songs like John Michael Montgomery. You should dance to this one with me," he says. Still leaning into the bar, he reaches his right hand across his left arm and gently takes my hand. "Please."

I look toward the bartender, and he offers me a sad half-smile that lifts just one corner of his mouth. I nod and carefully turn on the barstool so I don't catch my dress on the heel of my shoe before hopping down. Leaving my drink on the counter, Brian leads me away straight to the center of the dancefloor. "I'm not good at this," I say, just loudly enough that he might hear above the music. "I'm not good at new things."

Turning into me, he lifts my chin. His eyes are just as kind as they were a few hours ago in the church and I'm curious how someone can be such a gentleman in this day and age. I'm really not good at this ... at any of this.

"The most important thing is that you try new things. No one says you have to like them," he says, taking my left hand in his right and carefully stepping into me until his chest is a breath away from mine. His left hand slides along my spine until he holds it in place at the small of my back. Electricity wraps around my abdomen, my body excited by the closeness of another person. "By the end of this song, you don't even have to like me, because I'm new and scary, but you can pride yourself on having tried me on for size."

He begins moving his feet and I fall into step along with him. I haven't had a man dance with me like this since my father taught me the Waltz as a little girl. A smile forms on my lips of its own accord as the memory plays in my mind. I close my eyes as the scene unfolds before me and my legs do all the work without me having to count my steps. They just know where to go.

"Of course, if you like the way we fit, I would be more than delighted to dance with you for the remainder of the evening," Brian says, the words falling like leaves in autumn against my ear.

Opening just my left eye, I smile more broadly. The look on his face is nothing short of hopeful.

"So far, we seem to fit just fine," I flirt back. Amusement lights up his features and it makes me curious where Shana had been hiding this man. "How is it we've never met before, Brian?"

The song fades out before he can answer. He nods his head back toward the bar as the bass from the next song vibrates the wood plank floor. He raises his arm to get the bartender's attention, then orders me another Cosmo and himself a draught beer.

Taking a sip of my drink, I raise an eyebrow at him. "Well?"

"They're a couple. I'm not part of a couple. It's really as simple as that." He shrugs as if that's an acceptable answer. "Gavin started seeing Shana when we were in college at Syracuse University, and we did the group hangout thing where his group of friends and her group of friends melded into one big group. You know what happens after that?"

I shake my head.

He smiles, his nose crinkling just slightly. "Everyone else starts pairing up within the group and then it's just a bunch of couples. Unless you're the odd man out."

"You were the odd man out?" I'm truly shocked. Not only is Brian strikingly handsome, but he seems like a really nice guy. He must be a good person or Gavin wouldn't have asked him to be in the wedding. "How does that even happen when you look like this?" I wave my arm from his head to his toes. "Were they blind?"

His laughter calms my slight hysteria, likely ignited by the alcohol as it works its way through my bloodstream.

"I don't think they were blind. They just weren't who I was looking for," he says, and his eyes drop to the glass in his hand. The energy between us shifts. I feel a sadness wash over him for just a moment before he looks up and smiles at me again. "So, tell me, Emily, how is it you came to be friends with our lovely bride?"

I push aside the uneasy feeling, the one that tells me maybe his heart is spoken for after all. "Her dad lived down the road from me and my mom. We're not originally from here," I share. "After her parents split up and her step-dad's job relocated them here we kept in touch as best we could. Written letters and phone calls until the internet became a thing, you know? Shana and I spent our summers and some school breaks together in Mississippi when she'd come down to visit and when we graduated from high school I ended up in Michigan and she went to New York. We both moved to Tennessee after that."

"It sounds like you two have a pretty tight bond. It's hard enough keeping friendships alive after high school, let alone throughout an entire childhood of being separated," he says, and I don't miss the melancholy that slips into and around each of his words. There's a story there.

"It was difficult, but she was my best friend. She still is," I say. He looks at me, the question playing out on his face and I know what he's thinking. If we're such great friends, why am I not wearing one of those matching sky-blue dresses? "The only reason I wasn't up there with her today was because of a stupid boy. Sometimes, Brian, life just doesn't turn out how you plan."

He lifts his pint, allowing me to tap the rim of my martini glass against the side.

"Amen," is all he says before taking a long swig.

"Hallelujah," I respond. "Time to lighten the mood, sir. You owe me another dance."

We tip our glasses back, racing to the bottom, and set them on the bar simultaneously. He reaches for my hand and cautiously intertwines his fingers with mine. I feel the world fade away as he gently tugs me toward the dancefloor once more. I don't know the song, but I get caught up in the beat and his arms. It doesn't matter that my heart is cracked. He can be the salve to heal the wound.

For tonight.

Just tonight.

I let myself be swept away by Brian. Whatever memories he was replaying are forgotten as the evening becomes fueled by alcohol and the taste of one another. We've turned into that couple — the drunk strangers who can't keep their hands to themselves — but his lips find mine in dark corners and my hands fist his crisp white dress shirt inconspicuously beneath his suitcoat.

The only thing the carriage house doesn't have is an elevator for us to slip away to unnoticed. I want us to be unnoticed. This isn't something I want to explain to Shana tomorrow, how I came to the wedding single and coupled up with some guy I don't know. That's never been me, but, just this one time ...

One time.

We reach the top of the stairs and Brian turns to look at me. I don't miss the playfulness in his eyes as he takes my purse and places it beneath his arm, or as he takes my hands in his, pulling me down the hall until he reaches his room. There's a magnetism between us as I lean into him. His lips catch mine as I twist the doorknob and we slide together into our sanctuary for the night.

I close the door. Silently, I ask myself, "What are you doing, Emily?"

"I'm not trying to mend my broken heart in your bed," I say, as I press my back against the wall. I'm defensive without meaning it. It's easy to be defensive. It's all I've been able to be since Adam left and no one would take "I'm okay" as a legitimate answer.

The corner of his mouth lifts in a half smile, his dimple playing peek-a-boo with the scruff that's grown in throughout the day. "It's technically not my bed, so I'm okay with that," he says, dipping his head to place a kiss below my ear. Nipping my neck with his lips before looking me in the eye again, I can't ignore the tingling sensation growing. His blue eyes darken and, briefly, I see the serious side of Brian Stratford, as he says, "You don't be brokenhearted and I won't be the rebound. Tonight, we'll just be Emily and Brian."

I swallow hard before I find my voice again. "And tomorrow?"

"We'll figure it out tomorrow," he says. The warmth of his breath wisps across my lips and my tongue darts out to dampen them at the same time his mouth collides with mine. It's rough and wanting, and exactly what we both need.

Chapter 2

Emily

The sun creeping in through the window warms my face. His body curled into mine warms my back.

The throbbing in my skull, though? It's been a long time since I had a hangover and now I remember why I stopped drinking like I did in college.

Brian stirs behind me and then rolls onto his back, releasing me from a cocoon of arms and legs. I try not to move my head too quickly as I scoot to the edge of the bed. Sitting with my back to him, I brush the hair out of my face. Covering my bare chest, I stand and step away from the bed in search of my bra before remembering I didn't wear one.

I reach for my dress where he's laid it on the vanity beside the bed.

"What the fuck did you do, Emily?" I scold quietly as I come face to face with myself in the mirror above the dresser. "Idiot."

I pull my dress on. I use the bathroom and quickly wash my face. I search for my shoes.

This was my first and last one-night stand.

He was nothing but a gentleman. It has nothing to do with him as a person. I just feel ... wrong. This isn't the girl I am. I don't get drunk and sleep around. I have a good job and a great apartment and don't have time to try to start something with this man.

I've been sitting in a chair beside the window, staring at the toes of my shoes and contemplating how to make my escape when he says, "Breakfast?" I look up, and it all comes back to me how I ended up in that bed last night. God, he's gorgeous. "You look like you could use some bacon and French toast." And he's courteous.

The sheet slips off his chest as he sits up on the mattress. I look away, suddenly shy about seeing his body when he pushes the covers from his legs and climbs out of the bed. I glance at him as he pulls a pair of jeans on over his boxer-briefs and I watch the muscles in his back work together as he tugs a snug T-shirt over his head and down his abdomen.

I know exactly why I did what I did last night.

The heat in my cheeks is enough warning that I can't make this out to be anything more than what it was — liquor-driven lust.

The toes of his boots come into view as he walks toward the window and stands in front of me. He reaches down and takes my hand. "Come on. There's a little diner close by that makes the best sourdough French toast. The coffee is so-so, but it has caffeine."

Men like this don't exist. Where did he come from?

Brian glances at me every few minutes as we drive away from the carriage house toward town. He looks like he just walked out of an L.L. Bean catalogue, but I look like I'm ready to go out dancing. I catch him smiling as he stares out the windshield, and I want in on the joke.

"What's so funny?" I question, cautiously, and begin silently praying I didn't read this man all wrong and he's actually a serial killer.

"Nothing," he says, turning his head to look at me. "I just ... I had fun last night at the reception. I was kind of dreading it until I found you hiding at the bar."

"I wasn't hiding. Not really," I say. I can't contain my smile. "Okay, I might have been hiding. Weddings are just so awkward at this point in my life. I should be planning mine. Instead, I'm just attending everyone else's."

He pulls into a parking space in front of a building with the words "THE GREASY SPOON" splashed across the windows in vinyl. My nose curls slightly as I read the name of the business. Brian must have caught the look on my face because he starts laughing and says, "Don't judge the food by the name on the building. That's how you miss out on some of the best things in life." Brian reaches across the console, and gently squeezes my hand. "Come. We could both use food."

This sleepy town is just coming to life as we step from the car into a picture-perfect Spring morning. Brian meets me in front of the car, and we walk toward the building. He holds the door open for me and I start to take account of all the differences between him and the one before him. They are night and day, and I'm wondering why fate didn't let me meet this guy first.

I stop my thoughts. I don't have time to start something new when I'm trying to focus on my career now. It keeps getting shoved to the back burner and now it's the one thing I have to hang onto. The plan includes getting my life in order. There isn't room for a new man.

"What did you mean when you said you should be planning your wedding?" he asks once we're seated and have menus in hand.

I wasn't expecting him to pick up on that, so I take a second to gather my thoughts. How much am I willing to share? This was just one night. I'll just be a memory to him by the time tomorrow comes.

"I was in a pretty serious relationship. It didn't work out." I look over the top of my menu. He's laid his on the table. His gentle blue eyes are staring directly into my soul and I can't keep my mouth from telling him about my failed engagement. "So, there I was, backing out of Shana's wedding just weeks before it happens because I walked into my apartment to find all of his things gone. He was sitting at the kitchen counter and the only explanation he could give me was, 'I just don't think I want to do this.' He'd left our relationship long before that, but I thought we were working on it. I was wrong. He wasn't as emotionally invested in it as I was. I think he played along because it was making me happy. When he walked out that day, I realized I wasn't actually happy. I had been living in the memories of what were our good times. I wasted so much time."

"It wasn't wasted if you loved him. You had to have learned something from the experience of loving him to realize you weren't happy, even if it was after the fact," he says, lifting a cup of coffee to his lips. "It's acceptable to have those feelings and realizations. Once you admit it to yourself, you set yourself free."

I simply stare at him. It makes sense. Not once have my friends said anything about the entire situation to make me feel that it wasn't my fault. They've consistently called him names and threatened to slash his tires, but none of them have reminded me that life goes on or that I'm stronger than a broken relationship.

"Yes, I suppose I have learned from it. And I did love him. I still love who he is, I think, I'm just not in love with him. It's just difficult, you know? I've spent the last two weeks cancelling floral arrangement deliveries and reception plans. I spent months getting everything perfect for May twelfth, and now May twelfth is just going to be another Saturday."

"No, it isn't. Make it a day of celebrations," he exclaims, and I raise an eyebrow in his direction. "On May twelfth, you get yourself a fancy cake from a fancy bakery and a giant bottle of wine. Then, you eat that damn cake and drink the wine and celebrate the fact you are not entering into a loveless marriage that eventually will become filled with regrets. Celebrate the fact you won't raise babies in a home where their parents only tolerate one another, and instead give yourself a clean slate."

I bite my lip as I think about it. I could do that. I can find the silver lining.

"Take the next three weeks of what should be dress fittings and finalizing seating charts to grieve what you thought you had and then start fresh," he says with conviction. "Everyone deserves a second chance, even you."

I smile broadly. He's magical.

"This is the least awkward end to last night. Not at all how I pictured it when I woke up this morning."

"I'm glad I could be with you last evening and have the chance to know you better," he says.

"Where do we go from here?" I'm perfectly fine leaving this right here, but if Brian says he wants to see me again, I won't deny myself the opportunity.

"First, we're going to let this very nice lady take our orders," he says. "After that, we'll figure it out."

Chapter 3

Emily

May twelfth is in two days and I feel like I've been hit by a truck. I woke up and sprinted to the bathroom, called in to work, and have spent the rest of the day praying the nausea will stop soon.

"Shana, I'm supposed to be celebrating my freedom this weekend. I can't be sick. I can't even stomach the thought of looking at wine, let alone drink it," I whine into the phone.

"I'll be there in forty-five minutes with Gatorade and Tylenol. Are you running a fever? Maybe you have the flu," she says.

She's attempting to be helpful and I love her so much for that. I hate that she's going out of her way on the way home from work to mother me, but I've barely been able to get off the couch all day.

"I don't have chills or a fever," I moan. "I just can't stop throwing up."

The sea-sick feeling is constant.

"Let me Google your symptoms and get back to you. Regardless, I'll be there within the hour," she says. "I'm leaving the office in five minutes and will stop at the store on my way. I still have your key, so I'll let myself in. You go hug the toilet and I'll be there as soon as I can."

I push myself off the couch, feeling the urgency to move.

"I love you, Shana," I say, quickly, and hear her say it back as another strong wave of nausea hits and I drop the phone on the bathroom floor. I clutch the sides of the toilet and pray to God she hung up already and can't hear this.

I'm so tired that once it stops, I lay my head on my arm and cry. I haven't felt this sick in years. It's ruining my plans. All I wanted to do this weekend was eat cake and get drunk.

~*~*~*~

I'm not sure how long I slept with my face hanging over the toilet but, at some point, I curled up on the floor and used a bath towel as a pillow. I woke up to Shana brushing my hair off my forehead, her face scrunched up in concern.

"Morning, sleepyhead," she whispers. "Are you feeling better?"

My mouth feels like it's been filled with cotton and I can't make enough saliva to make it go away. My muscles ache and I have no concept of time.

I'm not nauseous, though, so that's an improvement.

"Maybe," I whisper back.

She picks up her phone and answers a call. "She's okay, Gav. It's pretty late, though. I think I might stay here to keep an eye on her. ... I will. I love you."

"How late is it?"

"Only midnight. You were sleeping pretty hard when I got here, so I didn't try to wake you and there was no way I was going to be able to carry you to your bed."

"You calling me fat?" I joke and close my eyes again when I see the smirk on her face.

"No, smart ass, because you're far from it. I'm just not good at dead lifting people." She sticks her tongue out at me when I open one eye to look at her. "Do you think you can move without getting sick or do you want to stay here?"

My hips hurt from laying on the ceramic tile but I attempt to sit up slowly. I'm dizzy, but it's not that bad. Definitely not as horrendous as the morning after her wedding.

"I feel hungover, but this isn't as bad as I remember that being," I say.

She stands and takes my hands as I get my feet under me. Pulling me up and steadying me, she cocks an eyebrow. "You hardly drink. When was the last time you were hungover?"

"Your wedding. It was bad. The only thing that cured it was bacon." I wrap my arm around her waist and she helps me to the couch.

"Bacon?" she asks. I nod. "Do you think that would help now? You're obviously hungry. Your stomach won't shut up." She laughs about it as she walks toward my small kitchen and grabs a bottle of Gatorade. "Seriously, if you think greasy breakfast food will help, I'll make it for you. I hate that you're sick right now. This was supposed to be your big weekend. New beginnings, right?"

Now that I'm not throwing up, I'm starving. I haven't wanted food this badly since the last time I tried to cut carbs. I would have stolen a slice of pizza from a toddler if the opportunity presented itself.

"I want to feel better than this. Make me all the bacon. I just bought some this week." She hands me my drink and turns back to the kitchen.

"Yes, ma'am," she responds with a swift nod of her head. "The morning after my wedding. Where did you go have bacon? How did you get home if you were drunk?"

She catches me off guard and I slowly lower the bottle from my mouth. "Uh, some greasy spoon near the reception hall."

Shana's head whips around. "That's nowhere near here, though. Where did you stay?"

"At the bed and breakfast," I say like it's no big deal.

"Em. Come clean. I know every single guest who stayed at the carriage house because most of them were in the wedding. You canceled your reservation. It's not that big a place," she says. She's holding my package of bacon in her hand like it's a hostage. I don't like where this conversation is headed. I didn't tell her about Brian because I didn't want to make it a thing. I just wanted it to be a nice memory. You know, one of those things I could think back on when I was having a bad day? She's going to ruin it. "Who did you stay with? Only two of the groomsmen were single and I only saw you dancing with one of them."

She already knows, then. My cheeks flare.

"Maybe I do have a fever," I say and attempt to stand.

"Oh my God, you had sex with Brian Stratford."

I freeze, not quite standing up, and look at her. She's wearing a goofy grin. I wait a beat — waiting to see if she has anything else to say — and then I slowly respond with, "Maybe."

"He took you out for breakfast. The guy can't even have a proper one-night stand without getting to know the girl," she says, smiling and shaking her head. She finally returns to the kitchen and then, over the half-wall, says, "I'm surprised. Neither one of you are the type to hook up. He didn't even do that stuff in college. But, if I had to choose a man for you to have sex with on my wedding night, it would have been him. He's just a genuinely nice guy."

Breathing a sigh of relief, because I honestly thought she might be mad about it, I shuffle over to the kitchen and grab eggs out of the fridge. "I want scrambled eggs, too."

"Getting your appetite back? That's a good sign." Shana gives me a sad smile. "If you're feeling up to it on Saturday, you should come over to our place. We're having some people over for a bonfire and beers."

I shake my head. "I think after this, I'm just going to stick around here and watch old movies."

"If you want company, I'll come over."

"Are you afraid of me being alone on what was supposed to be my wedding day? Because, really, I will be fine. I have lots to keep me busy. Look at all the room I have on those bookshelves now," I say pointing to the built-ins in the living room. "I just might go crazy and order a ton of stuff to fill the space."

"You're too cautious. You'd have to go to a real bookstore to make sure they feel right before you buy them. I know you, Emily, and with the one exception of banging Gavin's fraternity brother because you were drunk and vulnerable, you're a cautious person," she says. She begins laughing like she just heard the funniest joke ever, then says, "Even drunk and vulnerable, I'm sure you double-checked the condom was on properly."

My blood runs cold with the sharp realization that, no, that did not happen. My hand slowly stops whisking the eggs in my mixing bowl.

"Emily? Are you okay? You're really pale. Maybe you should sit down," Shana says, concerned. "I'll finish cooking."

She attempts to take the whisk from my hand, and I stare at her without relinquishing the utensil. I'm hanging onto it for dear life.

"You look like you're going to pass out. Go. Sit." She insists.

"Shana, we didn't."

"You didn't what?"

"He didn't have more than ..." I swallow. In my head I start counting the weeks. "Oh, crap."

"You didn't use protection?"

There's no grey area here and she can see the panic starting. "He only had one. We did it more than once." Her eyes widen and I know she knows where I'm headed. I quietly add, "The second time, I told him to pull out. He did. We were drunk, but I insisted it would be fine."

Shana slides the cooked bacon onto a plate covered with paper towels, washes her hands, kisses me on the cheek, and walks to the door.

"Where are you going?" I yell after her.

"The twenty-four-hour pharmacy. We're going to find out tonight if this is the flu or morning sickness. Cook those eggs. I'll be back in fifteen minutes to see if yours are fertilized," she says. Grabbing her purse and keys, she leaves without another word.

I start my normal process of overthinking the situation, trying to think of everything that could have made me sick, from things I ate to viruses going around this time of year … and I come up with nothing. There's only one logical explanation.

When Shana comes back into the apartment, I'm eating the scrambled eggs I made like it's my last meal. "I wasn't gone that long. You ate half the bacon already?"

"I'm starving. I was throwing up for an entire day and hadn't eaten since the night before," I say. "This could have been food poisoning. I ate soup from the Italian place up the road. They don't have a very good reputation."

"If it was food poisoning, you'd still be writhing in pain," she says, then hands me a box. "Go pee on this."

"This box has three tests in it."

"I know how much you like to make sure things really are as they are."

"What if I don't have to pee right now?"

She glares at me. "Get your ass in there and tell me if I'm going to be an aunt."

I hold the box up to my forehead and salute her as I walk toward the bathroom.

This is going to be the longest three minutes of my life, I think as I close the door. I pull the box open and grab one of the individually wrapped tests before sitting down. The instructions say to only get the test strip wet. "Who designed these things!?"

"Probably a man. Did you go yet?" Shana asks.

"Stop talking to me. You're making me nervous."

I recap the test and set it on the edge of the sink. I can't look at it, so I wash my hands and brush my hair. As I reach for my toothbrush, I glance to my left and there it is.

I hold the stick up to examine it closer.

After a couple more minutes, I open the bathroom door to Shana's expectant face.

"I think I'm going to need Brian's address," I say, quietly, the tears slowly coursing down my cheeks. I'm not shocked. I'm fucking terrified, though. "We made a baby."

Shana gathers me into her arms as I cry like I haven't cried in years. I cry on her shoulder until she leads me to my bedroom and lays down with me. I'm curled up in my bed, clutching a wad of tissues, with my best friend who doesn't know if she should be thrilled for me or not because I don't know if I should be happy or devastated. So, she just shushes me and tells me it's going to be okay.

I don't know if I believe her.

Chapter 4

Emily

The longer I wait the more difficult it becomes. I should have told him weeks ago.

I haven't.

The morning after I found out I was pregnant, I was gung-ho and ready to drive the hour and or so to Brian's apartment in Nashville. Shana told me to let the idea of being pregnant sink in a little first, so that's what I've done. In between hugging the toilet and eating crackers and bacon, I've gotten comfortable with the fact I'm pregnant. All I know about my baby's father is he's a nice guy who probably, with my luck, is in love with his high school sweetheart or the equivalent.

"Have you talked to him yet?" Shana asks over lunch. I stop chewing and look at her. "It's been five weeks. You should call him."

I move the food around in my mouth and mumble, "I don't have his number."

She blinks. "Why didn't you tell me you didn't have his number? I gave you his address weeks ago, but I figured you had at least exchanged telephone numbers." She grabs her phone, clicks a bunch of buttons, pokes at the keyboard, and then my screen lights up.

"Very mature," I say, reading the message. "'Stop being a miserable cow and call the man.' Is that really how you talk to a friend in crisis?"

"Em, I know this is difficult, but you're not going to go through it alone. Call. Him. I guarantee you, he's an amazing guy. He's not going to turn his back on you. That's not how he is."

I never said I thought he would deny this baby. The thought never crossed my mind. But what if he denies me? What if, despite being a nice guy, he hates me because I'm the one who made it okay to not use a condom? I don't believe for one second he would not care about his own child, but I don't think that automatically translates to caring about me.

"I'll do it this weekend. I have my first doctor's appointment and an ultrasound tomorrow morning. Maybe it'll be easier to give him the news if he can see it," I say. "I'm just worried, you know? We met at a wedding and had some pretty amazing sex, which has resulted in a very unplanned pregnancy. It just sounds like a setup for some cheesy romantic comedy … except it isn't funny."

I bury my face in my hands, unsure what my emotions are going to do. I don't like being in limbo.

"No, it's not," Shana agrees. "But, I'm pretty sure the little person you two created is going to be gorgeous and have a brilliant mind. I mean, you and Brian? Pretty good-looking couple."

I lift my head and glare at her. "Except we aren't a couple."

"Yet."

"I don't even know if he's going to want anything to do with us. It's a little far-fetched to consider us headed toward coupledom," I say.

Wiping my face with the cloth napkin, I begin to stand.

"Emily, I didn't mean anything by it," she says, concern marring her features.

I realize then I stood up and didn't excuse myself. She thinks I'm irritated, but in reality, "I just have to use the bathroom," I say. Laughing at her expense, I add, "You wait until you go through this. Now that the morning sickness has mostly gone away, I can't stop drinking and peeing. It's ridiculous. Oh, and I cried last night … because my toast was too toasted."

"Is that normal?"

"The stack of books next to my bed say it is," I reply as I begin walking away. "Hormones surging and causing all sorts of crazy things to happen."

Aside from Shana, my mom is the only one who knows I'm pregnant and I've sworn them both to secrecy until I've talked to Brian. It wouldn't be right for him to hear about it from someone else, which is why Shana can't even tell Gavin.

I'm in search of the restroom when the back of a blond-haired man catches my eye. The similarities in his build and what I remember of Brian's are uncanny. The way he stands at the bar talking to a waitress nearly has me detouring until he turns slightly and it's not him after all. Just another guy who looks an awful lot like him. I'd peg him for a sibling, except I don't know if Brian has any. My brain has been working overtime, and this is just one instance in a long list of them. A week ago, I thought I saw Brian at the local coffeeshop and found myself staring through the window at him until I realized people were looking back at me, which was more awkward than it sounds. The other day, I was fairly certain he drove past me as I was waiting at the crosswalk and I caught myself as I lifted my arm to wave to him.

Not telling him is starting to wear me out. I know Shana thinks I haven't attempted to contact him, but that's not true. I actually drove out to Nashville last weekend with every intention of talking to him. I sat in my car across from his apartment for over an hour trying to build up the courage to knock on his door. Then I saw him walk out of the building with a young girl who seemed over the moon excited to be talking to him. There wasn't anything indecent about it. The interaction was purely platonic in a big brother and little sister sort of way. She had a backpack slung across her shoulders with a baseball glove hanging off it. He was carrying his own glove and a bat. I was mesmerized watching them, watching him with a young person, and decided not to interrupt. They were playing catch at a park on the corner when I finally left for home. It was like witnessing a scene from the future.

Now that I have his phone number, Shana isn't going to let up. On Saturday, I'll make the drive again and this time I'll knock on his door.

~*~*~*~

The text message I send to Shana says, "I'm going to throw up. I don't know if I can do this."

I haven't been this scared in a very long time. I'm not even sure what I'm scared of. Rejection? Probably. I haven't seen or spoken to Brian since the wedding and now I'm showing up at his home unannounced. There are too many "what ifs" running through my head and none of them make me feel more at ease.

My phone dings with Shana's response. "You can do this, Em. I have faith in you. It's all going to be alright."

I lift my hand to knock on the door — 4C. I've double checked the address six times. I lower my hand without knocking and take another deep breath as I look at the sonogram picture in my hand. My nerves are shot. I hardly slept last night. I need to just get this over with so we can move on from here.

This time, when I raise my hand, I don't pause before the delivery. I hear a man's voice from the other side of the wood say loudly, "Quit your nonsense or I'm telling Mama," seconds before the door opens and I'm standing face-to-face with the one and only Brian Stratford.

"Why do you always resort to threatening me with telling Mama? I'm not a little kid anymore," the other man says. "Greg, talk some sense into him, would you?"

"You need to grow up a little, man," a deeper male voice says.

Brian stares at me as he loudly responds, "Because you're acting like a child." He lowers his voice when he greets me, though. "Emily, hi."

His smile puts me at ease and I trip over all the words I wanted to say. "Hi," I say back. I nervously play with my purse strap and bite my lip. "Hi."

"Hi," he laughs, swinging the door open a little wider and leaning against it. "What brings you all the way out here?"

I like that he doesn't question how I knew where "here" was.

A tall dark-haired man walks through the room behind Brian and before I can answer, a blond-haired man with a build similar to Brian walks into view. I consider the possibility that I'm going crazy, but I'm pretty certain that's the same man I saw in the coffee shop and at the restaurant. My mouth opens and then closes without any words coming out.

"Emily? Are you okay?" Brian asks. He takes my hand and tugs me into the apartment. "Tommy, can you grab her a bottle of water?" And the other man retreats to the room he'd initially come from. "You look like you should sit down."

"I'm sorry." Sitting down in the wooden rocking chair he's led me to I try to regain my composure, but I'm really bad at it and stutter through an explanation for my behavior. "I've just ... I've seen him up in Clarksville. It was a surprise, is all. I kept thinking it was you up there, actually. You look so similar."

"Yeah, he works up that way a few times a week," he says as Tommy walks back into the living room. "Emily says she's seen you around. Emily this is my brother, Tommy. Tommy, this is Emily. That's Greg. Greg, Emily."

Greg nods his head in acknowledgment but remains standing at the doorway to the kitchen. Judging by the look on his face, I get the impression I interrupted an important conversation between the three men. Tommy doesn't seem phased and reaches his hand out to shake mine firmly before handing me a bottle of water. I can't stop Brian when he tugs the ultrasound picture from the hand I was about to grab the damp bottle with. I'm pretty sure my life flashes before my eyes as time slows down and I watch him lift the picture out of my reach. A picture of his child. A child he still isn't aware he created.

I forget how to breathe.

"I'll hold that for you so it doesn't get wet," he says kindly. I watch as his eyes scan the picture before he moves to set it on a coffee table. I see the color as it drains from his face. He turns away from me, puts the picture closer to his face as he studies it, and then grasps the back of his neck. Softly, cautiously, he asks me, "You didn't just swing by for a visit, did you?"

"I'm sorry. I should have called you first. Shana gave me your address and phone number—"

He turns back to me and I see in his eyes exactly what I saw in mine the first night I was so sick. "Shana knows? Gavin and I play baseball every week. Neither of them said anything."

"I asked her not to. Gavin doesn't know. I wanted to tell you first."

When Brian doesn't say anything more, his brother asks, "Gavin doesn't know what?"

Brian and I both look at Tommy, and I then look at Greg standing in the kitchen doorway. I don't want these men I've never met before to judge me or Brian, but it's also not my place to ask Tommy and Greg to leave the room.

Brian must feel the same way as I do and says, "Guys, can you give us a few minutes?"

Tommy looks reluctant to leave, and I can't say I blame him. If I were standing in the middle of a conversation like this, I'd want to know what was going on as well. He doesn't fuss about his brother's request, but takes his time walking back to the kitchen as Greg steps backward out of the room.

Brian kneels on the floor in front of me, the picture still in his hand. Looking at what we made, he says, "This is a little person, Emily."

I'm so filled with dread and fear this won't end well that I can't even control my emotion and the tears spill down my cheeks. "I know. I'm so sorry." I cover my face with my hands, silently praying he doesn't hate me.

"We created a tiny person? We're having a baby?" His voice trembles.

I nod as I try to keep my sobbing to a minimum, but it's so hard. This is more terrifying than finding out I was pregnant in the first place.

"I'm going to be a dad," he says. It isn't a question. He's matter-of-fact about it. He's going to be a father and that's all there is to it. It speeds through my brain that he hasn't questioned if he's the father and I'm momentarily relieved. There's no question that he is. I hadn't had sex with Adam for weeks before he left and Brian was the only one after that.

He pulls me into his arms until I'm sitting in his lap on the floor, crying uncontrollably, and he simply holds me until the tears have stopped. In the end — after all the tears I've cried — his grip hasn't lessened, I'm exhausted, and the situation hasn't changed.

"I'm so sorry," I say one more time.

"For what? Last I checked I was there, too. It took two of us to make this baby," he says warily. "But how? We were careful."

"We were only careful once," I say, turning my face into his chest. "And once, we weren't so careful. Please don't hate me."

I hear him take a deep breath and then he wraps his arms tighter around me.

"I don't hate you, Emily. What do you need me to do?" he asks instead.

I shake my head and sniffle. "I don't even know. Exactly what you're doing right now works."

He laughs and presses a kiss to my temple. He makes it comfortable.

"How long have you known?" he finally asks and, when I tell him, he looks at me quizzically. "Weekend of May twelfth?"

I lift my head and slowly nod at him. "That's the one."

"Wasn't that supposed to be your clean slate celebration weekend?"

"Sure was. I couldn't even stomach the fancy cake and, for obvious reasons, I skipped the wine," I say. "I got pretty cozy with the interior of my bathroom, though. That was nice. I have some new decorating ideas."

He scrunches his face. Maybe talking about vomit isn't such a good idea right now. I'm past that and he doesn't need to live through it with me.

"It's gross, I know. I'll spare you the details," I say.

He helps me to my feet and gently places his hands on either side of my face. "You don't have to spare me the details, Emily. I'm in this with you," he says.

The determination in his voice makes me wonder if he thinks I would tell him I'm pregnant and then disappear. That isn't going to happen. Not now. Not after seeing his reaction.

"I'm terrified," I blurt out. "I have no idea what I'm doing and it's been information overload since I found out. This isn't how I thought life would turn out."

"Everything's going to be alright. We'll figure it out together," he says, but I don't ignore the worry in his voice or the concern in his eyes.

I just turned his entire world upside down.

Chapter 5

Emily

For the last few weeks Brian and I have met for dinner a couple times a week. We found a restaurant halfway between his apartment and mine that isn't very busy once the early bird specials are over. We've sat and gotten to know each other. He's the same guy who took me to breakfast the morning after the wedding. I don't know if I was expecting him to turn into an asshole, but that's far from the case.

Neither of us has tried to label what we are or what we're doing. Right now, we're having a baby with a side of dinner three times a week. We haven't defined anything. Tonight, he surprises me and out of nowhere says, "Are we dating? Is this what we're doing?"

I pause, my hand stopping mid-air with a French fry dangling between my fingers. Unsure how to respond, I stare at him until words actually form in my brain again.

"Is that what you want to be doing?"

I'm not entirely sure I'm ready to commit to a relationship again. Not that it's been easier being alone, but I don't want things to be even more complicated than they already are.

"Well, it would be nice to tell my mama that I'm meeting my girlfriend for dinner instead of referring to you as 'the awesome lady carrying my love child'," he says.

"You don't. Please, tell me you don't actually say that to your mom?" He responds by lifting his coffee cup to his mouth to hide a smirk. God, I love his smile. "I haven't even met her yet, so I would hope you have a little more couth than that."

"It's like you hardly know me. Of course, I have better manners than that. Tommy, on the other hand, that's questionable."

Tommy has been a sore subject. Since he works up my way frequently, we've run into each other around town. When I see him, I make a point of stopping and talking to him because I want to at least be on friendly terms with my child's father's family.

"He's not happy about us," I say. "I think he thinks I'm trying to trap you into a situation you don't want to be in, which, you know, I can understand.

Random woman shows up on your doorstep with an ultrasound picture? It sounds suspicious to anyone who wasn't there that night."

Brian folds his hands together around his mug and smiles at me. "He's jealous."

"You don't think he thinks what I think he thinks?"

"Nope. Tommy has been my sidekick for nearly thirty years. He's having a difficult time adjusting to me being needed elsewhere," he says. He rubs his hand along his cheek where he's allowed a bit of a beard to begin and then thoughtfully says, "But he won't admit that to me. Instead, he's just going to be mad about everything."

"Would he admit that to me?" Because I'm going to corner him when I see him next time, I silently add. It's not fair that he has a bad attitude about his brother's situation when it doesn't really concern him.

"If you give him that super scary look like you're giving me right now he probably would," Brian says with a nervous laugh. "Seriously, Em, it's kind of scary."

"I'm not a mean person. I just need you to know that. I'm not going to lash out at him," I say. "Not much, anyway. He was at the coffeeshop I go to when I went in yesterday and when I tried to place my order he changed it on me. Like, stood there and told the barista not to give me caffeine. At all. I hadn't even had a single cup of coffee yet."

Brian lets out a low whistle. "A man should not come between a woman and her first cup of coffee."

I pick up another French fry, put it back down without taking a bite, and push my plate away. "I just want him to accept me. He's going to be an uncle and he's treating me like I did this on purpose."

"He's overprotective, but I don't think he's purposely treating you that way."

Then why would he act like this, I wonder. He hasn't taken time to get to know me. Then again, Brian and I have hardly gotten to know one another. My mom told me to just leave it alone, move home, and raise this baby without telling him at all, but I would never have been able to do that. Any worry I had about him stepping up and being part of this baby's life was washed away the minute he knew. He's just as scared as I am, but he's happy. Brian is content with the idea of being a father, and it's made it easier for me to fall in love with the new life we've created.

"Earth to Emily?" I snap back from my thoughts. "Did I lose you?"

"No. I'm fine," I say defensively. "Are we still on for this weekend? Saturday dinner with your parents?"

He watches me closely before answering. "Are you sure you still want to do it? You've been nervous since I mentioned Mama invited you over and I don't want to put added stress on you."

"You're sweet, but I'm fine. I want to meet them," I say. "Just, do me a favor, and don't introduce me as your baby's incubator."

His smile wipes away the fears I have of coming face-to-face with the famed Mama Stratford. He slides out of his side of the booth and sits down next to me on mine, wrapping his arm around my shoulders and placing his lips to my head just above my ear. Quietly, he says, "So, does that mean I can introduce you as my girlfriend?"

He's perfect. He's everything I wanted in a partner. Maybe we didn't plan this, but he's part of my life for the rest of it, for better or worse, as long as this baby binds us together. I can't keep myself from worrying about the big picture, though. What if this doesn't work? What if after a while he decides to leave me, too?

It's a little late to be cautious, isn't it? We're past the point of being careful. I feel a blush rise on my cheeks and hear myself boldly say, "Yes."

Chapter 6

Emily

His voice booms behind me and I jump.

"Why are you always trying to feed that kid caffeine?"

I turn on my heel. My balance shifts and I start to stumble.

He grabs my elbows, but the touch is gentle, and he helps me stay upright.

All the kindness in the world won't stop my tirade, though. He's done it again and now I'm pissed. I push my index finger into his chest, my other hand going to my hip, and glare at him.

"Why?" I yell at him in the crowded coffeeshop. "Damn you, Tommy Stratford. Why are you always coming between me and my first cup of coffee? Are you stalking me? Are you the fucking coffee police now? Can't I just live my life in peace? No. You're following me around, taking away my opportunity to stay awake. This is the third time this week. Stop it already."

Backing away from him, I turn to the barista. She looks wholly confused and I tell her again what my order is. She gives me a nervous, "yes, ma'am," before moving to make my coffee.

When I turn back to him, Tommy is standing behind me, a dopey grin on his face.

"Why are you acting like such an asshole?"

He feigns shock, bringing his hand to his chest and gasping. "Me? I'm not an asshole. You're just bad at reading people." He nods toward the counter. "Coffee's up. Why don't you grab a table and we'll talk for a few minutes. Give me a chance."

I don't even respond. Rolling my eyes, I take my coffee and walk to the furthest corner with an empty table I can find. Fuming and feeling the rage build, I wait for Tommy to get his order and make his way toward me.

"You can't just feed my niece or nephew coffee. Here's a parfait and a muffin to go with it." He sets the food down on the table. I stare at it, not wanting to accept his culinary olive branch or whatever this is. The seat across from me scrapes along the stone floor as he slides the chair away from the table and sits down. "They say if you're going to drink caffeine while pregnant to do it sparingly. Instead of having a giant cup of caffeinated coffee, do half-caf and half decaf. It's in the books."

I lift my gaze from the food in front of me to his face, and the anger melts away a little.

"Have you seen my brother's apartment in the last couple of weeks? It's all pregnancy books, woodworking magazines, and books on starting businesses. I get bored when the Indians aren't playing, and I don't get into the shop stuff like he and Dad do. I have enough of my own marketing books to read and don't care to read his, too."

"So, you read the pregnancy books?" I ask, incredulously.

He shrugs. "I like to learn new things."

"And the following me around? Is that part of learning new things?" I question him while pulling the top off the muffin and taking a bite.

Tommy chuckles. I raise an eyebrow at him. "The top is the best part of the muffin," he says. He winks at me as he lifts his coffee and takes a cautious sip. "I'm not following you around, though. I'm trying to sell ads for the newspaper. I kind of hate it. I'd rather work for myself. I have today off, though, and was just trying to get more comfortable with my sales area."

I slide the bottom half of the muffin back across the table. "Peace offering?" I say, regretting my misjudgment. He smiles, a dimple just like Brian's appearing in his cheek. "I'm sorry for getting mad."

"And I'm sorry you thought I was being an asshole. I guess, if you don't know a person, it could definitely look that way. I promise you, I'm just trying to look out for you both," he says. Unwrapping the rest of the muffin, he pulls a piece off and pops it in his mouth. "I was jealous at first, though. Brian had talked about the girl he met at the wedding and all, but he left out the other details."

I see where this is going.

"You thought the baby couldn't be his?"

"It crossed my mind. I have pretty stellar hearing, though," he says. "It was pretty obvious to me and Greg he'd dealt his own hand when you corrected him about proper condom usage."

I smirk. "I threw caution to the wind once."

"That's all it takes. It should be the first lesson they have in high school health class if it isn't already," he laughs. "Forget talking about hygiene. Let's discuss how to put on a condom and pregnancy. Really scare the sex out of them with the birth video from the Eighties. No teenager wants to see that video."

"Sounds like you were one of those kids who paid attention in school."

"Like I said, I like to learn," he says, earnestly. "Tell me about yourself. It'll give you a buffer tomorrow when you meet Mama. She can be pretty ruthless."

I'm not sure how long we've actually been sitting here, but by the time we leave he's had two more cups of coffee and gotten me a sandwich. He knows a lot more about me, minus some huge details about a childhood illness. He started opening up to me about some of his fears, mostly about having a college degree but no real career path.

My opinion of Tommy Stratford has drastically changed in a matter of hours and as I walk back into my apartment, I send Brian a text message. "Your brother is a good guy."

It doesn't surprise me when my phone lights up and it's Brian calling. "You gave him the death glare?"

"I yelled at him in public. I might have scared some of the other customers."

He laughs and while I wait for him to regain his composure, I start to see the humor in it all.

"I'm glad you two talked," he says, finally. "The last thing I want is for either of you to hold a grudge."

"No grudges," I say. "He was just doing what he thought was the right thing."

"Was it?" he asks. When I fail to respond, he asks again softly, "Was it the right thing?"

Tommy's looking out for all of us. He's not his brother's shadow, though he feels like that's what he's been most of his life. Tommy's heart is huge and I think as time goes on, I'll be eternally grateful for the friendship he and I formed today.

"Yeah, I think so."

I can hear the smile in Brian's voice when he says, "See? Everything's going to be alright."

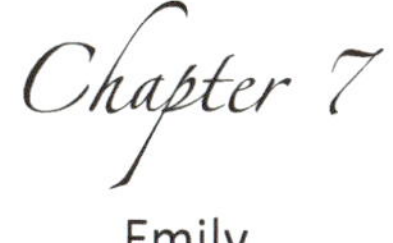

Chapter 7

Emily

When tomorrow comes, I'm a mess. I get to Brian's early so we can get ready for me to meet his parents. He said everything would be fine, but I think he lied to me. My nerves have me all tangled up.

"I look like I haven't slept, Brian. They're going to wonder what the hell you were thinking ending up with me," I say, looking in his bathroom mirror.

I didn't take time to put makeup on before coming into Nashville, not that I wear much more than eyeliner and lip gloss. Grabbing my overnight bag — his idea, because if we get back late he doesn't want me driving all the way to my place if I'm exhausted — I reach for my face wash hoping something as simple as the peppermint scented liquid will calm me down. Nothing else has worked so far.

I look in the mirror again and he's standing with his shoulder against the doorframe while watching me.

"What?"

"Mama's had kids. I think she'll understand if you look tired," he says. "Pregnancy insomnia."

"Someone other than Tommy has been reading the pregnancy books, I see. So, tell me, Dr. Stratford, is this just how my face is going to look forever now?"

"Only for eighteen or so years."

I try not to smile, but a laugh sneaks out. "Smartass."

Don't let yourself fall in love with him, I tell myself. I don't know where the thought comes from, but it seems like a rule I want to break.

"We need to leave in about ten minutes. I'll go start the car and get it cooled down while you finish up in here," he says, catching my eye in the reflection before backing out of the door and away from view.

I wash my face quickly so I don't hold us up, and when he walks back in the apartment he finds me staring at the living room wall. I'm mesmerized by the photos he has framed and scattered around. I've never seen a single man's home so put together, and certainly not one that has pictures from his life scattered about in some purposeful manner. There's one in particular, slightly right of middle, that's caught my attention and I feel my chest tighten.

He notices where my eyes have landed and answers the question I hadn't yet asked.

"That's me, Tommy, and Stella. We were living in New York," he says. He's in the middle of a memory and I feel like an intruder. "She was my best friend. I haven't talked to her in years, though. Long distance friendships don't always work out. Mama keeps in touch with her parents sometimes, but Stella and I haven't since we were in middle school."

"She's the one." I say it as fact. There is no question in my mind that this is the girl he was remembering the night we met, the reason for his melancholy. He doesn't correct me or question what I mean, only stares at the picture a second more before blinking away the emotions attached to the memories.

He clears his throat as though he's trying to remove the remnants of her name. "You ready? The car should be cooled down by now," he says.

I watch him push his hands into his pockets as he begins to walk away, the slight downward turn of his shoulders making me wish I had never noticed the picture in the first place. I want to ask him how a love can last that long without being near her. I choose to ask him if he's okay. Instead of words, he turns back to me and reaches for my hand. As though nothing happened, he kisses me on the cheek before leading me down the hall.

We sing along to the radio on the drive over to his parent's house. He asks me about my next doctor's appointment. I ask him about his job. By the time we get there I wonder if I merely imagined the way he reacted after telling me the little bit he did about the girl in the photo.

As we pull into the driveway, I recognize Tommy's car and am thankful he's already here. Brian brings us to a stop. I sigh deeply as he puts the car in "park" and cuts the engine.

"There's no reason to be nervous. They're human. No cyborgs here," he says, trying to make light of the situation. "I promise, Mama is probably going to ask you for your life story and then talk your ear off about babies and all the stupid things I did as a kid."

I bite my bottom lip to keep it from trembling, but it doesn't stop the tears from building up in my eyes until they spill over. Brian touches my chin and tugs gently until I turn my head.

"Why the tears?" His concerned eyes look into mine and I know he cares, he cares so deeply about me and this baby, but I'm still so scared that I'll develop emotions bigger than I can handle. Bigger than just caring about him because he's my baby's father. We've decided to give a relationship a chance, but I keep trying to stop myself from falling for him. I'm afraid of the future.

"I—" I stop. He brushes the tears off my cheeks, his concern growing deeper. "I'm scared."

"There's no reason to be afraid of this. I'll be right here. I'll always be right here, Emily." He leans across the console and catches my bottom lip between his, briefly, before pressing his forehead against mine. "I'm not going anywhere."

I nod my head, accepting his promises. Wiping the tears from my face, I reach for the door handle. It's now or never, I say to myself, and step from the car.

His mama meets us halfway between the house and where we parked. She tips her head to get a better look at me as she gets closer and I watch her face fall slightly, the broad smile that crinkles the corners of her eyes disappearing.

"Emily? You've been crying. What's the matter?" she asks before turning her attention to Brian. Placing her hands on her hips, she scolds, "What did you do? This poor woman is carrying my grandbaby and you go and make her cry in the driveway? I raised you better than that."

Brian and I both attempt to speak at the same time, then stop.

"I did not make her cry, Mama," he says, matter-of-factly. "Things are just overwhelming."

I can't think of a better way to describe it, so I don't elaborate.

"Well, of course it's overwhelming. You're going to be parents," she says, but laughs heartily. "You're never going to know what it means to be underwhelmed again."

This isn't how I pictured meeting Brian's mother for the first time would go. I assumed there would be a period of warming up, but there's nothing cold or awkward about it and I can see where Brian and Tommy get some of their personalities.

"I'm Kathryn," she says. Pointing to a deck off the back of the house, she adds, "And that's Ben. We're so happy to finally meet you. The boys have told us so much, but it's nice to be able to put a face with the name."

I don't know how it happens, but I find myself wrapped up in her arms and she's giving me the best hug I think I've ever received. She squeezes the insecurity out of me, leaving me comforted and loved on a level only a parent could take me to and I wonder how hard I'm going to have to fight myself to not fall for all of them.

~*~*~*~

It's dark outside before our visit comes to an end. Kathryn ran me through the gamut with questions about my childhood, my family, my pregnancy, and by the time we've eaten and gone through Brian and Tommy's photo albums it's well past nine at night. I think if we gave ourselves the option we would stay even longer.

Brian finds me on the deck. I went to the kitchen to put dessert dishes in the sink and snuck away to welcome the evening while sitting on a porch swing hanging on the deck. Taking in the sound of crickets and bullfrogs in the distance and the sight of stars twinkling above us, Brian catches me yawning. It's a quiet moment and my mind has slowed down just enough to let the tired seep back into my bones. He sits down beside me and pulls me close. I turn away from him so I can lean back against his chest and kick my legs up to stretch along the swing. It's comfortable. The entire day has been a whirlwind, but one I would repeat again and again if I could.

"I didn't think your parents would be so accepting of me," I admit to him. "This has been a lot to take in and process."

He wraps his arms tighter around me and kisses the top of my head.

"Mama's kind of amazing like that. She doesn't judge much, but she'll pry for information until she knows everything about a person," he says.

"And your dad?"

"Dad's the silent, thoughtful type. He's taking it all in and when he's ready he'll make his feelings known," he says. "He's actually pretty thrilled about having a grandbaby."

I open my mouth to say something, but then let it go. My mom isn't exactly thrilled, but she's not mad either. I didn't follow her advice and since telling her I wouldn't be moving home to raise my son or daughter without a father, she's been somewhat indifferent. I expected more from her and I'm having a difficult time understanding her lack of emotion. She asks me how I feel when we talk once a week, but things have been strained.

"We should probably head back soon," he says close to my ear. "There's no way you're driving back to your place tonight. I'm not even sure you'll be able to stay awake long enough to get back to my apartment."

We haven't spent a night together since it happened and the memory sends a tingling sensation down my spine. That frightens me. It's dangerous enough being sexually attracted to him, but our situation is leading me down a path of emotional attraction I wasn't looking for.

"Do you think that's a good idea?" I ask, genuinely curious.

"You can have the bed. I'll sleep on the couch," he says. It's as though he knew where my thoughts were headed.

I turn on the swing and face him. Before I can stop myself, I say, "You don't have to sleep on the couch."

His eyes open a little wider, one eyebrow raised. He smiles as he places his hands on either side of my neck and tugs my lips toward his. My mouth opens slightly to welcome the softest kiss I could imagine. My heartrate picks up and I don't want his lips to stop.

But they do.

"We need to go," he whispers. "Like, right now."

I nod my head vigorously as he stands and grabs my hand. Yelling through the open window, he says, "Mama, we're heading out. We'll drive safe. I'll call you tomorrow. Love you!"

"Love you, too!" I hear her yell back through the window as we rush to the car.

The drive back seems to go on and on, but when we pull into the parking lot of the apartment it feels like it was all too short. Brian parks, kills the engine, and gets out to open my door. It's surreal as he takes me by the hand and we walk into the building as though we've done this a hundred times and it's a natural occurrence for us.

The elevator ride to the fourth floor is torture as he places his hand to the small of my back and I lean into the sneaky kisses he trails up my neck. He finds my earlobe and I let out a low moan. He smiles and, as if on cue, the elevator stops. He applies just enough pressure to my back to make me move and I'm grateful his apartment is only a half-dozen steps away. I wait for him to put the key in. He can't get the door unlocked quickly enough. My back is pressed against the wall, my chest heaving slightly in anticipation of what is about to happen. He glances at me and all I see in his eyes is desire.

The night we met replays in my mind. I laugh out loud as the door swings open.

He grabs my hand, pulls me inside, and slams the door shut with his foot.

Chapter 8

Emily

The smell of fresh baked pastries, coffee, and bacon pulls me out of the heaviest sleep I've had in weeks. It takes me a few seconds to open my eyes as I lay and simply enjoy the feeling of being rested. When I do open them, Brian's in the doorway holding a mug of steaming coffee. His hair is still damp from a shower I didn't hear him take. He's dressed in torn jeans and a snug fitting superhero T-shirt and, in an instant, he steals away my breath.

The longer we stare at each other, the quicker I lose this battle. The one where I don't fall in love with him in the end.

"Good morning," he says. A smile plays on his lips as he brings the coffee mug to his lips and blows gently across the top. "There are fresh muffins when you're ready."

He bakes? Why is he perfect?

"And bacon," he adds with a smirk.

"I love bacon," I say, rolling onto my side and closing my eyes again. "That's the only thing I wanted to eat the first few weeks. Breakfast foods are the best."

He doesn't say anything, but I hear him walk closer to me and set his coffee down on the nightstand. The bed shifts as he climbs in again beside me. I open my eyes and he's mirroring me on his side of the bed.

He offers me five simple words that have a bigger impact than I think he'll ever realize.

"I should have been there."

"You didn't know. I was too afraid to tell you," I say quickly and regretfully as though that will make it easier, but find myself reaching out to touch his cheek. "We agreed it was one night, Brian. It was only supposed to be one night. We were so sure we wouldn't see each other again we didn't even exchange phone numbers."

He turns his head and presses a kiss to my palm.

"But I shouldn't have let you agree to that. Even if we hadn't ended up pregnant, I could have at least been a friend to help with all the crap you were going through," he says. "I should have been there, Emily."

"You're here now," I say, trying to quiet the pain he feels. It wasn't just his decision to leave the prospect of "us" at that diner. I agreed. I wasn't looking for more. That was then, though. "You are here right now, and that's more than I could ever ask for. You're present and active in this baby's life. You're in my life. It doesn't matter what we decided back then. What matters are the decisions we make going forward."

Neither of us expected the offer of breakfast to turn into such an intense discussion, but in the end, we both needed to have this conversation.

"Going forward," he repeats. "What's the next step?"

"I have no idea." I laugh, then groan. "I think before we talk about that I need to get out of this bed and have my one cup of coffee for the day."

He kisses the tip of my nose and helps me out of bed. Before he walks back to the kitchen, he bends and places a kiss low on my abdomen. He speaks softly against my skin, his breath tickling the small bump that's begun forming.

"You're a pretty lucky kid to have her as a mama. We're a couple of fortunate guys to have her in our lives."

Running my hand through his hair, I say, "But what if he's a she?"

"I'll love her just the same." He stands and looks me straight in the eyes. I hold my breath as he breathes in deeply, his eyes damp with unshed tears. "I didn't know I could love someone so much before I've even met them. It's a lot to take in."

"Just think how you're going to feel once he's here," I say.

"What if he's a she?" Touché.

I lean in and kiss his cheek, brushing my face against his stubble and loving the feel of it on my skin. "Then I'll love her just the same."

He pulls me tight, chuckling softly, before letting me go. He turns and rounds the end of the bed, grabbing his coffee on the way out the door, and says, "Bacon's getting cold and I'm going to eat all the muffins if you don't hurry along. We've got a busy day ahead of us."

We do? We hadn't made any plans that I was aware of, but when I come out of the bathroom and make my way into the kitchen I see what's on his agenda.

"So, I thought we could go shopping. Babies need so much stuff," he says. I begin thumbing through the catalogues and printout pages from various shopping websites. "Did you know they make a thing called a wipe warmer?"

"When did you do all this?" I don't hide the shock in my voice. He's literally looked up everything we might need. The baby isn't even here yet and he's already Super Dad. "I haven't even thought about any of this beyond the fact we'll need two car seats."

Brian hands me a cup of coffee and looks at the table as I pick up a quilt pattern that's laying on top of a pile on papers. I'd know that pattern anywhere.

"You're planning to make a quilt?" I ask, catching his eye.

He shrugs as if to say, "So what if I am?"

"My mom made nine patch quilts every time a gift giving occasion arose. It's her favorite pattern," I say, still holding the paper in my hand. "You're actually going to quilt a blanket for our baby?"

He plucks the page from my hand and turns it around to study it.

"Not exactly. Mama gave me the pattern last night and asked for us to pick out fabric. I was thinking reds and greens, you know, since you're due right after Christmas." I'm not sure what my face is saying, but I think he reads it wrong. As he hands the paper back to me, he cautiously says, "Or not. We can pick any colors you want to."

"I think I'm in love with your family," I blurt out and then laugh nervously. His eyes grow wide and I see the questions forming in his mind. I didn't say I was in love with him. "I don't have a ton of extended family, Brian. I have my mom and Shana and a couple friends from college that keep in touch irregularly. This is all new to me. Is this how you live every day? With so much emotion and support? How do you handle it?"

He pushes his hands into his back pockets and leans against the counter. He studies me thoughtfully before coming to a conclusion.

"One day at a time, Emily. I've never not known family to be like this, so to me and Tommy this is normal. You need life advice or a recipe or a tow because your car broke down, you call your family. If it's too much, I can ask Mama to tone it down. I'll just warn you, if I do that, she's going to take it as a challenge and up her game. This place will end up filled with pies and cookies and knitted things before you know it," he says in all seriousness.

I'm not used to this at all. I've been on my own, relying on myself since I left for college. I needed to get away from the smothering, because that's how my mom showed love. Overbearing smotherer. I know why she was that way, and sometimes continues to be. Having a kid with cancer made her that way. I don't talk about it. I overcame it when I was barely into high school and have been in remission since. There's no need to dredge it up, so I'm not going to.

"Reds and greens are great. I love Christmas colors," I finally say. What else can I say? I may have only just met her, but I would never want to risk hurting his mom's feelings by asking her to back off. It's comforting to know she wants to be so involved, even if it's a tiny bit overwhelming. I look back to the table and take a leap of faith. One day at a time. "Maybe we can start by looking at cribs and carseats today. Save some of the smaller things for another day?"

Brian nods. His smile doesn't quite reach his eyes. He's treading carefully as though I'm fragile and I don't like that. I smile back at him, because he's wonderful and thoughtful and cares so deeply about what we're going through. Pushing up onto my tiptoes, I kiss his cheek.

"Let me jump through a shower and get dressed, then we'll go, okay?"

He nods again and places his hands around my coffee mug. "I'll keep this warm while you get ready," he says, his voice low and hoarse. It reaches into my heart and squeezes a little bit tighter.

Chapter 9

Emily
Week 22

"Hurry up! We're going to be late!" I yell to him from the door.

He broke down my defenses and I finally agreed to move in with him a few weeks after I met his parents. It's a hike to work, but his apartment is a two-bedroom and larger than mine was. My lease was up; he just renewed his. It just made sense considering the circumstances.

It's only been a month. We're still adjusting.

"We are not," he says, scrambling to the living room from the bedroom. He came home late, so now we're running behind. There's shaving cream on his temple still and a hand towel thrown over his shoulder, but he shoves his feet into his boots and ties them in record time. He stands and walks to me while wiping the cream from his face, then tosses the towel into the rocking chair. Pulling the door open as I glare at him, he says, "See? Not going to be late."

He presses his hand into the small of my back and pushes me gently out the door.

My emotions are everywhere lately. Some days I want nothing to do with him. Other days I text him ninety-seven times before lunch and then get mad when he doesn't respond right away. I know he's busy. I know he has responsibilities other than me and the baby, but this is hard. I don't know what I'm feeling most days and I don't have a lot of people to talk to about it. I don't see Shana nearly as much anymore because of the distance. We talk semi-regularly, but I haven't gotten to visit with her like I used to. We meet for lunch once a week and things are different. Plus, she and Gavin are wrapped up in each other as newlyweds should be. I feel my friendship slipping away and I'm not even sure I want to reach out and hold onto it. I have Tommy, though. Brian's amazing, despite my inability to focus my feelings about him, but Tommy has been a rock for me. He probably didn't think he'd become that person when we first met, but the more time he spends with me when Brian works late, the more important he becomes to me. He's slowly beginning to replace Shana. He's becoming the brother I never had and I talk to him about nearly everything, except for my hot-and-cold feelings about Brian. He sees it. I don't have to talk to him about it when he's seen me go from lovable to miserable in the blink of an eye.

I promised myself I wouldn't fall in love with Brian, and I'm certain that's why my head is all over the place. It's not fair to him, but I don't want to love someone who can't love me back. He loves me because I'm carrying his baby and he loves me because I'm smart and funny, but he doesn't look at me like I catch him looking at the pictures on the living room wall. As much as I want to be it for him, I push him away unless there's a carnal need. The physical attraction is there. We haven't denied ourselves to one another. But when we share the bed every night, we wake up most mornings still on our own sides instead of curled into one another in the center like we did for the first couple weeks.

"We're going to hit traffic," I say, under my breath, as I walk toward the elevator. "This is the most important ultrasound, Brian, and you let yourself get caught up helping someone else. Again."

"That's my job, Em. To help people," he says, trying to hide his irritation. "I had no idea that meeting was going to go as long as it did. Some people have no direction when it comes to their client base. That's why they hire me."

When we first met and he told me he was a problem solver, I had no idea what that meant. Now, I understand "small business consultant" is a synonym for not coming home for dinner because everyone else is more important.

"Plus, if I take a ton of time off before the baby is born, I'll have no time to take off once he's actually here," he says.

It doesn't make me feel better.

"I just want this baby to be important to you, too." It was a low blow and I know it's a lie that the baby isn't important to him. I know it hurts him just as I intended it to as soon as the words leave my mouth, but I can't take it back. I look away to hide the shame I feel for hurting him.

Why am I pushing him away? What good does it do me? I ask myself those questions all the time, but I never hear an answer. I just feel guilt and go to bed with a heavy heart.

He doesn't hold my hand like he usually does and when we get to the ground floor, he steps out of the elevator ahead of me. He walks one step ahead of me the entire way to the car. Instead of opening my door, he goes to the driver's side and opens his own first but then stands there staring at me, and it's the first time I've seen Brian angry. Not just a little irritated.

Seething and hurt has replaced the easy-going man I sleep with every night. He clenches and unclenches his jaw, gripping his keys tightly in the fist he's made and rested on the roof of the car.

"Do you really believe this relationship and our baby isn't important to me? Do you, for one hot second, think I would turn my life upside down if I didn't care?" He speaks sternly, and I realize how very little I know about Brian. "My dedication to you and our child runs deep. If there's one thing you shouldn't question, it's that."

Without another word, he gets in the car and starts the engine.

We don't talk on the way to my appointment. The radio is turned off. Silence. And it drives me crazy until we're pulling into the parking garage and I finally say, "I don't question it. Not about the baby."

"You did," he says immediately.

"I'm not trying to. I'm stressed out and lonely. This is all new," I say, and he looks at me with an expression that tells me he thinks I'm forgetting he knows. "To both of us. It's new to both of us, Brian, and I have no idea what I'm doing. I'm angry one minute and the next I'm overcome with fear or elated or ... pick an emotion. I've probably felt them all in the thirty minutes we've been in the car."

I'm surprised when he reaches across the console and squeezes my hand. It says, "I'm here and I'm your friend and I'm in the trenches with you." It doesn't say, "I love you." He's never said, "I love you."

And neither have I.

~*~*~*~

"What are you hoping for? Boy or girl?"

The ultrasound technician has been trying to make idle chit-chat since I laid down. I don't really enjoy small talk, but this question I can answer in more than a single word.

"We just want a healthy baby," I say to him. I stretch my neck and twist to see the screen. A tiny fist opens and closes beside a tiny cheek and a button nose. We see and listen to the heartbeat.

"I think that's what everyone wants," he replies while measuring a femur. "Are you hoping to find out sex today?"

I turn my head and look at Brian, but he isn't paying attention to me. He's locked onto the screen, watching his son or daughter wiggle around and I think I see the moment it hits him. I witness the very moment it becomes real to him that he's going to be a dad. He's been excited and nervous, he's seen my belly grow and felt the baby move, but this is different.

He lifts his hand to his mouth as if to hold in the emotions, but his eyes speak freely. He's head over heels in love with this child.

"Brian?" I say to get his attention.

He doesn't pull his eyes from the monitor. "Yeah?"

"Are we finding out what we're growing in there or waiting?"

He looks at me finally and I wonder for a split second why I feel so compelled to make sure it won't work between us.

His voice is scratchy, but I hear him say, "I want to know."

Brian carries the strip of photos when we walk out of the radiology department and head over to my doctor's appointment where everything is routine and normal and happy. He asks about childbirth classes and the nurse pops in to hand him a schedule of upcoming sessions. He's been involved as much as he can be, which I'm thankful for, and is caught up in the pictures of our son after all the regular questions are asked. He's not paying attention to us when my doctor mentions having lab work done before my next appointment, but she's discreet and doesn't say specifically what they're checking for.

But I feel my heart skip a beat because I know what they're checking.

I don't want to think about it.

I can't think about the possibility, so when we get back home I take a warm shower ... and I pray.

Chapter 10

Emily
Week 30

"So ... how's things?"

I refill Tommy's coffee cup while trying to ignore the question. We've both somehow managed to have a day off during the week and he arrived with breakfast as Brian was leaving for work. Brian is understanding of my friendship with Tommy, or at the very least he hasn't questioned it. There's nothing romantic about our relationship, nor would Tommy attempt to make it something it's not.

"Things are okay. I think. Maybe?" I'm really not sure. "We've had some pretty deep, heartfelt conversations about us, you know. I don't think either of us knows how long this is going to last, if it lasts at all, but it scares us both to think about not co-parenting under the same roof."

"You going to marry him?" he asks when I hand him back his coffee.

"Who said anything about marriage? That's not even a topic that's been up for consideration, Tommy. Brian isn't in love with me and, as much as I hate to admit it, I'm not in love with him," I say. "I think any love we have for one another is concentrated in my uterus. That's where our love for one another is. We're friends, though, and it's nice to have his support as a friend as well as Britton's father."

Tommy begins to say something and stops himself.

"What?" I ask, but he shakes his head. "Tommy, you don't have trouble expressing your opinion, so spit it out."

"But y'all keep having sex. If you don't love each other, why are you sleeping together?"

I bite back a laugh. He's serious.

"Because it feels good. Because we're physically attracted to one another. Because my sex drive is through the roof," I say. "Not to mention, we're in a monogamous non-romantic relationship. He's not going to be bringing random women home and I most certainly am not looking for a man. Our situation is unconventional, Tommy, but we're content. It works for us, so we're taking it one day at a time."

Pulling a chair out from the table, I sit with my knees touching his. I grasp his hands and force him to look at me.

"What's going on with you, T?" He's been acting off the last couple weeks and I can't put my finger on it. "Why the sudden wonder about what's happening to my relationship with Brian?"

"I don't know. I'm scared you guys won't stay together or you'll move back home to Mississippi to be closer to your mom and take Britt with you and he'll never see us again. You're my best friend, Emily. I don't want to lose you," he says.

"Why would you think I would leave and take the baby with me? You aren't going to lose me, Tommy. We're family," I say.

He breathes in deeply and reaches up to touch my face. "I just feel like ... I feel like something is going to take you away and I can't shake that feeling."

I laugh it off. He doesn't know about me beating Leukemia when I was a kid and I've kept it from him that my oncologist sent me for bloodwork a week ago. It's routine. Everything has been normal and routine. Tommy shouldn't be worried because everything is going to be alright, and I tell him so.

He pulls me into a hug, but he's treating me like I'll break if he hugs me too hard. I squeeze him tighter. I want to push all these worries he has right out of his mind and fill him up with nothing but good thoughts.

"We should go shopping. Didn't you say the other day you have a date this weekend?" I say when I sit back from his embrace. "Let's go find you a new dress shirt or something."

"You just want an excuse to shop and make me look presentable," he says, leaning back in his chair again and draining the remains of his coffee.

"What if I do? There's nothing wrong with treating yourself once in a while. You can't wear the same clothes you wear to work if you're going to take her to a fancy restaurant." I stand and hold my hand out for his mug. "Besides, you work with her. She's seen everything in your closet. There isn't much in there to begin with, and if you plan to start interviewing for better jobs it would benefit you to have a few new outfits. You need to get a haircut, too."

He laughs as I turn and set his cup in the sink, but the smile fades from my face when my cell phone rings and I recognize the area code for Biloxi. Tommy begins to say something as I pick the phone up from the table. I hold a finger up to hush him as I answer.

"Hello?" I say.

On the other end of the line I hear my cancer doctor ask if she's speaking to Emily Long. I slowly feel a cold creep over me as she begins to explain there were irregularities in my bloodwork. Tommy gives me a worried look and I cover my mouth as I turn my back to him.

"Emily, I've been going over your labs. Your white blood cell count was pretty elevated. We'd like to repeat your blood work before getting too worried, though. I know, this isn't the call you ever wanted to get from me. Usually I call to tell you everything is good." She sounds as grief-stricken as I feel. "I've known you since you were twelve. I know what you've been through. Let's take the proper precautions to ensure your health and the baby's."

"When do I need to come back?" I ask, careful not to speak too loudly or openly.

"You don't need to come to Biloxi yet. I've already talked to your obstetrician and she's sending a lab slip in. Can you be there for the follow up blood work tomorrow?"

"Yes, I can be there tomorrow. Thank you," I say.

"I'll talk to you in a few days. In the meantime, let's just think positive thoughts," she says. "It could be nothing."

Chapter 11

Tommy

She picks up her phone from the table and, holding a finger up to hush me, answers it.

"Hello? ... Yes, this is Emily." She listens. I watch as silent horror fills her face and she covers her mouth, before turning her back to me. She speaks quietly, asking, "When do I need to come back? ... Yes, I can be there tomorrow. Thank you."

The phone call ends. She places the palm of her left hand to her forehead and cups her right hand around her belly.

"Em? Everything okay?" Of course, everything isn't okay, but I don't want her to think she has to tell me. I phrase it as a question so if she doesn't want to talk to me about it she can brush it off with a simple statement like Brian does. He's been really good lately at asking me to mind my business. Emily usually gives me information when I ask questions. She's an open book.

She doesn't turn to face me. Instead, she brushes her hair back from her face and, even with her back to me, I can see she's wiping her fingers beneath her eyes. A smile is plastered to her face as she pivots on her toes to face me. It falters despite the positivity she tries to put into the words she speaks. "Yeah. Yeah, Tommy. So, shopping? Are we going?"

I stare at her from the table where I sit. The smile wavers as a tear slides down her cheek and I feel my gut twist. Panic grips me and I start firing questions at her. "Emily, is there something wrong with the baby? What's going on? Do you want me to call Brian?"

"No! No, don't call him. The baby ... that baby is fine," she pleads, and I see the defiance in her face. "He's perfect. He'll be absolutely perfect."

Standing, I walk to her and grasp her shoulders in my hands. I tower over her and she refuses to lift her eyes to mine. I feel her arms as they begin to quietly quake, as the first painful cries are ripped from her chest. She falls into me as her body heaves out her pain, and I simply hold her. I'm not sure what else I'm supposed to do, so I just hold her like Mama used to hold me after a bad dream and I let her cry. She doesn't tell me what happened or who was on the phone. I don't pry. She'll tell me when she's ready.

Chapter 12

Emily

It's been two weeks since my labs came back the same. I'm exhausted, but we don't know if that's just pregnancy. Brian thinks I've just gone back home to visit my mom since she isn't planning to come up to Tennessee in January when Britt arrives. But really? I'm sitting in a procedure room at my oncologist's office with my mom. I just want to get this over with.

"How have you been feeling?" She's been quiet since I pulled in the driveway yesterday. I'm a coward and didn't tell her why I was coming to visit until I got here. We haven't seen each other since well before I got pregnant and now things just feel tense. "You look tired, Emily. I wish you would have flown. Or had your boyfriend come with you. You shouldn't have driven all that way alone and I can't imagine he wouldn't want to support you through this, too."

I pick at the imaginary lint on my hospital gown. "I didn't want him to come."

"What do you mean? I know I haven't met the man and you're afraid to let me, but why wouldn't you want him to be here?"

"I don't want to talk about it, Mom," I say. When I lift my head, she opens her mouth to say something then stops. I think she figures it out, so I just say it. "He doesn't know I had Leukemia. He doesn't know any of that medical history. I don't talk about it. I don't want to talk about it. I don't want people to pity me."

Her jaw drops slightly and I see the hurt in her eyes — how hurt she is for me because of what we've already been through and how afraid she is that we're going to go through it again. Mom doesn't pity me. She's always told me how strong I was during that time.

"I haven't told him about any of this and I don't want to. If it's back, it's going to take me this time."

"Don't say that. Please, Emmy, don't say that." The unshed tears glisten in the fluorescent light as she stands from her chair in the corner and walks to me. She lifts my face until my eyes meet hers and she's defiant. She's adamant. "If it's back, we're going to beat it. You have a baby to raise. You're stronger than this disease. You're the strongest girl I know and don't you forget it."

Chapter 13

Emily

I spent four days with my mom and never heard from my oncologist.

It's day nine and my phone is ringing. I know the number but don't want to take the call.

Nine days.

"Hello?" I answer apprehensively. My office door is closed, but I still lower my voice as if that will make this conversation disappear.

"Emily, do you have time to talk?"

I feel the dampness on my face and watch as tears drip onto my blotter in slow motion. It's early. We can start treatment now with little to no side effects to the baby. A small percentage. A tiny chance of something going wrong.

"No." I say it without thinking. What is there to think about?

"No?"

"I won't start treatment. Not right now. I won't take the chance."

"That's your right, Emily, but we need to consider everything," she says.

"I am considering everything. We wait until after he's here." I'm determined. They aren't pumping me full of chemicals until after he's out and safe and I've gotten to spend a little time with him.

My doctor remains quiet on the other end of the line. She sighs. "You're stubborn."

"I know."

"We're going to keep a close eye on you."

"Like a hawk. I know," I say through my tears.

"I'm going to be a thorn in your OB's side. If there's any radical change between now and your due date, you need to prepare yourself to deliver early," she says. "The goal is a healthy you and a healthy baby. You're my focus, though."

When we hang up, I call my mom. She answers on the first ring and as I tell her the news, we cry until we have nothing left. I text Brian and tell him I'm working late. I text Tommy and cancel our plans to watch movies and talk about his failure to launch.

Instead of doing anything, I sit in my office and drown out the world.

Chapter 14

Emily
Week 36

"Emily? Hey, Em, wake up." I open my eyes slowly. Brian is sitting on the floor beside the bed, gently running his fingers up and down my arm. "It's after ten. Are you going to get up? Tommy and Mama are here. We were going to go out for brunch to make our Christmas plans."

I'm so tired I can hardly drag myself out of bed. I force myself to sit up, and it takes work. It's a struggle, but I tell myself I can get through this. Everyone says you're exhausted at the end and then get a huge spurt of energy. That's what this is. It's the final push to finish growing a human.

I apologize for sleeping so late. His brows knit together, worry permeating his beautiful features, and I hate that I'm making him feel that way.

"Do you want to go with us, or stay home and rest?" His voice is full of empathy. The end of my pregnancy hasn't been restful for him. I've caught him sitting in the living room in the middle of the night, reading and planning a business he wants to start. He always tells me he can't sleep when I ask him if he's coming to bed.

"I'll come with you. Give me enough time to get ready and we'll go?" I offer him a smile, the best I can muster, and pull myself from beneath the sheets.

"When did you get that?" I look to where he's pointing and see a large bruise on my thigh.

"I walked into the corner of a desk at work the other day," I say, touching the angry purple mark on my leg. "I must have bumped it harder than I thought."

"It looks really painful, Emily. Should you have it checked out?" His concern is palpable. I feel it crawl into me and I almost tell him why I'm bruising so easily.

Instead, I say, "The doctor is having me take extra iron already. I'll bring it up at my appointment next week."

I need to start being more serious about taking the supplements I was told to buy. Maybe then I wouldn't look like I'm already dead. For the time being he seems satisfied with the answer, meekly smiles at me, and moves on.

"How are you feeling aside from tired?" He places his hand on my abdomen as Britt begins moving around. He's been head down already for the last few weeks, so all we've been able to feel are knees and an itty bitty tush. Despite everything else going on in my life, my pregnancy and focusing on Britton have helped me hold onto my sanity. It's kept the idea of dying from creeping in and taking over. Thinking about all the wonderful things he'll do as he grows up with Brian as a father has saved me from the crippling depression that could be consuming me.

"Hungry and emotional. Right this second, I'm feeling more hungry than emotional, though," I say. I lean into him and he wraps me into a hug, one like he hasn't given me in weeks. "I know things have been difficult, Brian. But I hope you know how grateful I am to have you in my life."

Every day I try to pull him closer while pushing him away. I need him to know, despite what our future holds, he's been a blessing to me.

He breathes in deeply, pressing his cheek into my hair, and says, "I know. I just worry that I'll never be enough."

I pull back to look at him. "What do you mean?"

"It keeps me awake. Thinking about us and not us. Thinking about Britt and how I fear I'll never be a good enough dad. I'll never be a good enough friend," he says. "Don't you ever worry that we'll move on and he'll be the only reason we keep trying? I'm scared I'm going to mess up my relationship with him and he's not even here yet."

Oh, Brian, no, no, no.

"Fear is normal. Remember? I would be worried more if you weren't afraid of all that. That's what parenting is, isn't it? Being afraid but doing it anyway? This is something we'll get through. Everything is going to be fine," I say, hoping he can't see right through my lies or sudden bout of bravery. "Everything is fine."

~*~*~*~

"So, we've got Brian's coffee cake, Mama's collection of pies, Dad's doing the turkey, I'll bring my amazing good looks, and Emily wants to make the potatoes," Tommy reads from the list we've started putting together while waiting for our meals. "Shouldn't we have things like green beans and stuffing, too? I feel like we've had green beans in the past."

I scrunch my nose.

"No? No green beans," Tommy says, raising an eyebrow, and scratches it from his list. "Spinach salad, then. The one with bacon, cheese, and hard-boiled eggs? Yeah?"

I smile but roll my eyes. "Does it taste better than it sounds?"

"So much better. You'll love it," Tommy says. Mama chuckles lightly under her breath.

Brian and Mama are talking about things we need to finish before the baby is born but, aside from a few uttered words here and there, the table is silent once our food is served. Chatter about putting the crib together doesn't keep me from thinking about the very real possibility that this could be my last Christmas. I know my mood shifts, and I know Tommy can feel it from across the table.

He taps his shoe against mine and my head jerks up. "What was that for?" I ask quietly

"What's with you?"

"Nothing is 'with me.' I'm just deep in thought," I say. I can't even convince myself that it's nothing so I know I'm not fooling him either, and he narrows his eyes at me. "I promise. I'm trying to prepare myself to push a small human out of my body. That's all. Is that okay with you?"

Mama and Brian haven't said anything but, when I snap at Tommy, Brian puts his hand on my leg. It's not possessive and it isn't a warning. It's a continuation of his concern from earlier this morning but this time, I don't want it.

"I'm fine, I swear," I say, quietly, before excusing myself and standing up from the table.

My appetite is gone and I just want to get out of here, but I can't escape Tommy. As I walk away, I hear Brian say something before a chair is pushed back from the table.

"No, I'm not going to just let it go. I upset her. I'm checking on her," he says, and begins following me toward the restrooms. His footsteps come up behind me quickly. "Emily, wait!"

I round the corner to the bathrooms, out of sight of our table, as Tommy reaches out to grab my arm. When I turn toward him, he takes one look at me and pulls me into his arms. "What is going on with you, Em? You can't tell me something isn't up when I've been watching you for weeks on this downward spiral. It's getting worse. You're withdrawn. You canceled plans with me twice last week and Brian said you worked late the other days. We're all worried about you."

I don't know what to tell him, so I tell him as much of the truth as I'm willing to share. I tell him about the sadness, the anemia, the worry that I'll have to deliver early because it's just something to worry about ... but I never mention the cancer.

"You can count on us to help you through this, Emily. You aren't in this alone," he says. "Listen to me, we're going to do Christmas next week and it's going to be the most amazing Christmas ever. I'm going to make you that stupid spinach salad and you're going to keep taking the iron like you're supposed to. We're not going to worry about meeting this kid early because babies come when babies are ready, right? Right."

He talks more like he's trying to convince himself than me, and that's okay.

"This sadness? It's not going to win," he says. Taking my face in his hands, he's determined to make sure I know how he feels. "You are so important to me. You and Brian are my best friends, and nothing is ever going to change that. But this sadness? You can't let it settle in for the long haul. It's not part of the you I love, and it needs to leave."

"It's not always that easy, Tommy," I say. "What if it stays?"

"What if it doesn't?"

Chapter 15

Emily
Week 38

The begging has started. The doctor in Nashville who's been monitoring me closely for my oncologist in Biloxi was the first to tell me I need to consider delivering Britton now so I can begin treatment.

I told him not yet. He said I was an idiot for waiting. I told him he was no longer my doctor and called my oncologist back home.

"You know, I don't take kindly to being called stupid in any form, so how about we just do it my way?" I say when she calls me back. "I'll consider delivering early if it's necessary. It isn't necessary yet, is it?"

"It's getting to that point. How's your energy level?" she asks.

I've bounced back some. I'm not sleeping for sixteen hour stretches like I was a few weekends ago. Brian and I have been washing baby clothes and, while I'm ecstatic to meet our little boy, that sadness definitely hasn't gone away completely. It permeates everything I do. I wash receiving blankets, and then cry as I fold them. I sit in the rocking chair in the living room when Brian works late and imagine what it will be like when I'm gone. I'm watching my life unfold like I'm merely a spectator trying to distance myself from the crowd.

"It's good," I say. "I've got energy."

I leave out the part about makeup covering the dark circles beneath my eyes. As far as Brian knows, I'm well rested. I can lie through the phone like a champ. She asks about my next prenatal appointment. It's in three days, I tell her. She says she'll talk to me after that.

When we hang up, my attorney looks at me from across the table. I've moved beyond the other four stages for the most part, and now I'm firmly planted in "acceptance." I know what my fate is. I can feel it so deeply that I don't even question it. Since I'm not going to dwell on dying, I'm going to focus on getting everything ready for Britt.

"Are you sure you want to do this, Emily?"

"John, this is the only thing I'm absolutely certain about. Just make sure when I'm gone, after all my funeral expenses are paid off, everything goes to Britton."

Any money I have will go into a trust for Britt.

"But you want to relinquish your rights to your son without talking to his father. I'm not trying to change your mind, but this might be difficult to do," John says. "I don't know if a judge will grant this or do it quickly."

"I can't let my son watch me wither away. I won't make Brian take care of me and a newborn. I'm not asking you to get this approved. I'm telling you to do it. I'm dying, I know I'm dying, and I don't want to feel like I didn't give Britt the best chance at having the best life even without me in it. Make it happen. Please," I plead with him. "I don't want anything to hold Brian back from moving on once I leave. I don't even want him coming to look for me. Terminating my rights to Britton is the only way to make sure that happens."

It doesn't even matter if the chemo works. I don't want to make someone go through this with me. My mom will. She's done it once before. We both know my odds, because I'm waiting, likely aren't good. If the cancer doesn't kill me, the treatment probably will.

When I get to the apartment, it's early evening and Brian isn't home yet. I know I threw it in his face once before out of frustration, but since then I don't get upset about the long hours he's putting in. He's sacrificing time now to have time later.

He's going to need time later.

I need the time now.

~*~*~*~

It jars me out of a deep sleep. The sound of Brian talking carries through the open bedroom door from the living room, but I can't make out the words. Quietly, I push myself off the bed. His words are slurred. The alarm clock on his side of the bed reads "3:37" and I hope I'm not being overly brave when I take a deep breath before walking out of the room.

Standing with my shoulder against the wall, I watch him as he holds a picture in one hand and tips a bottle of beer against his lips with the other.

"I was going to come find you," he says. "I was always going to come back and now I can't."

I know what picture it is. It solidifies my decision to leave. It makes it even easier knowing once I'm gone maybe he'll go find her ... maybe he'll be able to love her like he can never love me.

"Why did we lose each other? I drove home once when I was in New York. I was going to find you then, but it didn't feel right," he says, solemnly. "So, I drove back to Syracuse and decided to wait."

"Why did you wait?" I ask, my voice barely above a whisper.

When his eyes meet mine in the dimly lit room, I might as well be here to collect his soul the way he looks at me.

He's broken.

He's trying not to blame me.

He's failing miserably.

"Why did you wait so long, Brian?" I ask again. Realizing this conversation may not be remembered tomorrow, I press on. "You were kids when you moved here, but you've loved her so much all these years. You should find her. Even if it's just to have your best friend back, you should find her."

"I should find her." He's drunk, but I hear the resolve in his voice. "I waited because fate had other plans, I guess."

I laugh, but we both know it's not funny.

"You know what my dream was, Emily?" He smiles, wistfully, looking at the photograph again. "I was going to work down here and save up all my pennies. Then, when it was time, I was going to move back to New York and open a coffee shop. Or maybe a bakery. I wanted that small-town life I remember from when I was a kid. I wanted everything to be perfect before I looked for her."

I step closer to him as emotion floods his features. My heart begins to break for him and all I can hope for is that Stella is sitting somewhere thinking about him, too.

"What if she isn't there?"

"Then at least I'll still have a cool business and the small-town life," he says. Draining what's left of his beer, he sits down in the rocking chair and stares at me. "But that isn't going to happen now. I won't give up time with my son to chase a dream."

"You wouldn't be." He doesn't hear me say it because he's already moving on to the next part of the conversation. Or, if he does hear me, he ignores it.

"Why are you encouraging this? It's mean," he says.

"Because maybe chasing that dream will be exactly what you need," I say. "Don't make me explain what I mean, Brian. Just ... believe in fate when she's talking to you."

He watches me as I brush the hair from my face and cross my arms under my swollen chest. I cross my feet and uncross them. I don't want him to give up what he was working for because he has a child. I will be gone. I don't want him to blind himself to the possibility of having all those things he wants because his focus is solely on raising Britton.

Each time he blinks, he opens his eyes a little slower. The bottle hanging from between his middle and forefinger wiggles free as his body relaxes. I walk over and pick up the bottle, carry it to the kitchen, and place a quilt over his lap before returning to bed.

Chapter 16

Emily
Week 39

I'm closing in on my due date and they're all seriously discussing induction. I'm seriously considering it and it weighs heavy on my heart as Mama Stratford helps me put the final touches on Britton's room.

His crib is ready for him. There's a dresser filled with clothes and diapers and extra packs of wipes. I bought a small bin for the toys Tommy and Brian have already bought for him. Brian built and hung a rack for baseball bats, mitts, and balls even though Britt won't be mobile for many more months. Brian has thought of everything he can to make bringing a baby back to this apartment the best experience ever.

But he hasn't thought of everything like I have. I've bought canisters of formula to have on hand because as much as I wish I could stay and be his source of food, I know I won't be able to do it for long. I'm mentally preparing myself for all of these new things that I'll give up almost as soon as I get to experience them. My mom is patiently waiting for the phone call that he's arrived and then we'll plan for when I leave. No one at work knows what's going on. I'd like to keep it that way for as long as possible. I know once I start hitting my insurance, someone is going to have questions.

Thinking deeply about everything I need to finish, I didn't realize how closely Brian's mother had been studying me. Not until she closes the door and speaks.

"You don't have to tell me, but I know. I can see it. I've seen it a hundred and more times. Just tell me how bad it is. That's all I ask."

"Know what?" I ask, painting on the best smile I can. It's pointless. I see it on her face — the sorrow, the sympathy. My mouth goes dry. I open it to say more but nothing comes out.

"You haven't told Brian or Tommy, have you? My boys would have said something to me before now if you had."

I shake my head.

"Come, sit," she says to me, and motions to the armchair in the corner. We bought it for middle of the night feedings. I don't even know why when I won't want to let him out of my arms until I absolutely have to. "Emily, I'm retired now, but I was a nurse. The boys never told you, I'm guessing, because I never talked much about it. It wasn't one of those jobs that had happy endings. Most days were hard."

"You were a nurse?"

She nods her head. "I worked for Hospice."

My voice is gone. There are no words. I can't lie to a woman whose job it was to care for people like me. The empathy reflecting in her eyes tell me she's seen this too many times already and instead of pitying me, she's hurting alongside me.

"I won't tell them, Emily, if those are your wishes, but at least let me know you have a plan. Are you going to try treatment?" she asks, carefully weighing her words.

I nod slightly, and say, "I've waited so long, I don't know how much time I'll have even with chemo. I've waited so long, I don't know if it's worth fighting it. They caught it early, but ... I couldn't risk something happening to Britt. I never would have forgiven myself. Not if I lived through it and his health was compromised."

She squeezes my hand. It's full of strength. It's comforting.

"You have made the best decisions you could make for you. You've put him first." Kathryn takes a deep breath, pulling back the emotions that are just beneath the surface, and gives me a scared smile. "You didn't have to take this on alone, Emily. Once Britton is here, though, and you start treatment, you aren't going to be able to keep that from Brian."

"He won't know. I won't be here."

She cocks her head to the side, the questions playing out on her face in the way she looks at me. I watch as it registers.

"I've already made the decision to stay as long as I can, and then I'll be leaving for Mississippi," I say, barely able to hold my tears in check. I stumble through the explanation about meeting with an attorney and giving up my rights to Britton once I leave. She's understanding, but not. She's worried I'm being irrational but agrees that I'm being logical. She doesn't judge.

"I love you like my own child, Emily, and I wish there was something I could do to convince you to stay. I wish you'd let us help. What can we do to make this easier? What can I do to help?"

It's the first time I've seen Brian's mama vulnerable and I hate knowing I'm the one who put her in this position.

"You will be helping. I know you will, Mama, because Brian's going to need all the support he can get while he raises this baby alone," I say.

She holds her words. She doesn't try to find a way to make me stay. She pulls me into a hug like the first time I met her and the rest of the world falls away as she pushes her energy into me, as she weeps into my hair, and promises to help bring up my baby to be a gentleman like his daddy and uncle.

Chapter 17

Emily
Week 39, Day 4

I finally agreed to the induction. My doctors want me to have the energy to deliver and reduce the chance of needing surgery. He's ready to come out, even though he's trying to convince me otherwise. We need to be at the hospital early and I can't sleep, so I'm writing to him. Someday he might have a chance to read these words.

Dear Britton,

Today is my induction date. You're supposed to come out and meet me, but you seem fairly comfortable where you are tucked up under my ribs.

When I was a teenager, I never thought I would be able to have this moment. I truly believed my chance to be a mother would be stolen from me and it wasn't until I beat cancer the first time that I allowed myself the chance to be ... just, be.

I wanted to be a teen. Then I wanted to be a college student and be an adult. I wanted so badly to be a mom, but there wasn't ever the right person to take on parenting with me.

Then I met your father and in one evening he made the stars shine brighter. Without even trying, he made me feel like I was the most important person he had ever talked to. He had a way about him that simply put me at ease. He made me feel cherished when that was the last thing I thought I would find ... and that's how we got to this point.

Now, we are waiting for you.

Love,
Emily

Brian wakes just as I'm crawling back into bed. He rolls over toward me and places his hand on my belly, and I wonder what it would be like if I was able to stay. What would we be like if I had told him I'm sick? How would that have changed us? Would it have changed? I don't want to doubt my decision but in sleepy moments like this it's difficult to leave alone the questions in the back of my mind. He's never mentioned the night he opened up about wanting to move back to New York, and I don't want to try to remind him about it. But I have talked to his mama about it. There are things Brian doesn't know. Mama keeps in touch with Stella's parents regularly, she just doesn't mention it to him.

Sometimes, I just want to tell him, "Stella's married, but she's not happy. She works too much and he's not the world's best son-in-law. Take Britt and go to her." But I won't. Mama says it'll happen when it's meant to happen and I trust her completely.

As Brian drifts back off to sleep, the weight of his hand getting heavier, Britton moves a little. Wiggling and squirming and once he's comfortable, he stops. I feel my eyes grow heavy and finally, sleep consumes me as well.

~*~*~*~

"He's perfect." The words escape him as a whisper and a rush of relief washes over me. Britton lays on my bare chest, quietly listening to my heartbeat from the outside for the first time, as Brian places soft kisses to my sweat-drenched forehead. It's January 15. We're officially parents. Watching Brian watch our son in awe is my undoing. He whispers again, "He's so perfect."

Dear Britton,

You've finally made your way to my arms. When it was time to arrive, you came quickly. Your first breath, the first time I heard you cry ... you're fierce and strong. I didn't know how proud I could be of someone who was only minutes old.

Today is the greatest day of my life all because of you and you don't even know it. My only hope is that in the brief time I'll hold you, you will feel my love and know it will never waver. I want to wrap you up in it like a warm blanket and I want it to be around you always. Someday, when you become a parent, you'll understand. As I sit here and watch you sleep peacefully, I can't help but wonder what your life will be like when I'm gone.

I haven't told your daddy yet that I'm leaving. I'm not sure when I'll go, but I'll give you every ounce of my love before I do. It's been difficult the last couple months trying to hide away my feelings, knowing I'm lying by omission. No one knows the cancer is back except for your Grandma Kathryn. She's kept my secret and, while I shouldn't be ashamed that she has, I have so much guilt that she made the promise not to tell her own son. She doesn't understand why I've made the decision I have, but she respects my right to make the decision. That's more than a lot of people would give me.

I hope you never think I left because I didn't love you or your dad. I did and still do. My love for your dad is complicated, though. He has such a beautiful heart — he opened it up to me the night we met, he gave me pieces of it when he found out you were growing in my belly — but it has never been a gift he could give me to keep forever. I'm not sure if he knows that. I'm too afraid to tell him.

Love,
Emily

Chapter 18

Emily
Britton: One Week Old

The last week has been difficult. The pain from delivering a baby subsided quicker than I expected, but the surge of emotions hit hard. I try to hide away when it hurts — when I look at his face and know I won't be here to watch it change from the baby he is to the little boy he'll soon be and eventually into the man he will become.

Brian has caught me more than once curled up in the middle of the night with Britton as I'm crying into his hair. I see the sad look he gives me when he thinks I'm not paying attention. I'm exhausted and I know he's worried, so he tries to get up in the night when I get up and he takes the baby when I need to sleep. If I wasn't dying I would be eternally grateful for those kind moments. Instead, it feels like I'm sacrificing time with him. That's not fair to Brian. It isn't fair for me to want to keep Britt all to myself knowing Brian will have him forever ... not when Brian doesn't know I'll be gone soon.

It's been a week of watching and knowing. A week of putting off planning to leave. How much longer until I can't bathe in that newborn baby smell?

Dear Britton,

You're one week old today. We've been home for a handful of days, most of which I've been fortunate enough to spend snuggled up with you. You nurse, we nap, I change your diaper, and we repeat the cycle all day. I feel like I've been blessed beyond measure. Your dad has been attentive and given me time to rest while he takes his time cuddling you. He says you look a lot like me, but your Grandma Kathryn has showed me pictures of when Daddy was a baby. You'll grow up to look just like him and Uncle Tommy.

Part of me wishes I could stay here with you forever, but it simply isn't possible. I look at the calendar and wonder how many more days I'll get to stay before it gets to be too much. How long do I have until he notices I'm more than just tired? Knowing how I feel now versus how I felt last time, I have a week or so left with you. It's not anything I want to think about, because thinking about it detracts from my ability to be fully present with you.

Eventually, I will have to give you a bottle. I'll have your dad do it because I'm afraid I will cry. It'll be his chance to bond more with you, but for now I'll let you nurse. I'll give you the best of me for as long as I can until I have to begin my long goodbye.

Love,
Emily

Chapter 19

Emily
Britton: Two Weeks Old

Dear Britton,

It's been a glorious two weeks with you. I try to keep my tears to myself, but it's getting more difficult. I know it's almost time for me to go.

Your dad keeps catching me hiding away as I cry. He did a wonderful job educating himself on everything from pregnancy to birth, and it's apparent he also did some extensive reading on postpartum depression, because he thinks that's what this is. I know he means well, I know his heart is in the right place, and someday he will understand. Someday he will look back on the first few weeks of your beautiful life and realize all my tears and all our little arguments were because I knew what he didn't. For now, I try to reserve my sadness over leaving the two of you for when I shower or he's gone to work.

I love you with all my heart, but my soul is getting tired.

Love,
Emily

~*~*~*~

"Emily?" he asks, standing in front of me before leaving for work. He squats down and touches my knees as I rock gently in the chair in the living room. I don't stop rocking. "Em? Do you think we should call someone?"

I've cried for three days straight. I feel my time getting close. I know it's coming, I just don't know how long it'll take.

"For what? I'm fine," I say. Britt is sound asleep against my chest. He stirs and lets out a yawn as I reach forward and touch Brian's face. I'm going to miss him. I made myself not love him, and now I regret not giving us a better chance. What if I had told him? I still could tell him.

"You cry all the time. I'm worried about you," he says.

I won't tell him.

"It's a lot to take in. I'm trying so hard. What more can I do?"

I didn't think he could look more worried for me. He's read every one of those damn books. He's trying to fix it and this is something he can't fix.

"Let's move the chair over by the window," he suggests. "Maybe some sunshine will help?"

He's trying so hard, I tell myself again, and I comply. What harm could come from sitting by the window?

Once Brian leaves for work, I carefully get up and place Britt in his crib. I take the notebook back out from between the mattress and box spring where I've hidden it. I just wrote to him last night, but the words don't stop. I've been penning letters to Britton in it since before he was born and there are more to write. I don't know if he'll ever read them, but it gives me closure to leave him messages. I reach into my bag and search blindly for a pen. That's when I see the small blue velvet bag laid atop an envelope on my nightstand beside the bed. My name is written in Brian's neat lettering, all capitals. I love his handwriting.

Cautiously, I open the card first. The simple statement on the front catches me off guard. "I love you ...," it says. The phrase neither of us has ever uttered. I open it and take a cleansing breath as I read in his writing down the center of the card:

For all the things you gave up
For all the things you gave us
For the person you are
For the person you've become
For the child you bore
The son you gave me
The family you've sacrificed for
Because you're my friend

I love you ...
Regardless of the sorrow.

We've never told each other, "I'm in love with you," and, while I know that's a huge declaration and one I don't think either of us will make unless it's truthful, I need you to know how much you do mean to me. It's been hard. I wish I could fix it for you. I hope you know how much Britt needs you

... how much I need you. We may not be in love, but we have love for one another. I'm glad I get to parent with you. I'm glad I get to know you. Britt and I are blessed to have you.

Love,
Brian

The tears drip down my face. I finally pick up the little velvet bag and open the drawstring. Tipping it into my hand, a delicate silver chain falls into my palm. An infinity symbol stares up at me. Britt's birthstone is placed perfectly in the center. Brian's and mine surround it.

I should have let myself fall in love with him ...

Chapter 20

Emily
Britton: Three Weeks Old

My mom and I spoke yesterday after Brian left for work. She heard it in my voice. It's time to go.

Dear Britton,

I've made plans to leave. I'm weaker than I thought I would be at this point. I thought I would have more time, but I don't.

You're so little still, and I know it'll be years before you really notice I'm gone. I've already made the decision to give up my parental rights. I don't want your dad to think I'm leaving and will one day come back and try to take you. I wouldn't do that to him. I don't think I'll be around in order to do that anyway.

Believe me when I tell you that it's not that I won't fight the cancer — I'll be going home to visit your Grandma Long and will begin treatment once I meet with my doctor — but I don't think this is a fight I can win again. I waited because I wanted you to be unscathed. You're my perfect little man and I'm so beyond grateful to have had this time with you regardless of how short a time it's been.

You've nursed less and less in the last week, taking more bottles than not, so I know you'll be just fine eating for your daddy. You'll grow to be a big strong boy. Maybe you'll play football or have your dad's love of baseball. Maybe you'll decide you want to be a dancer and be the star of your recitals. It doesn't matter to me what you become as long as you find your happiness and always are gentle and kind.

Kindness matters, Britt, and that is one of the many lessons I have learned from your father. His kindness has shone through the arguments we've had, arguments I know would be resolved if he knew the reason I've become withdrawn. I'm not proud of myself for leaving, but I can't make him be responsible for a new baby along with caring for me. It isn't fair to either of you. So instead, I will treasure his kindness, his love and generosity, and I'll go.

Love,
Emily

Chapter 21

Emily
Britton: Three Weeks, Two Days Old

I haven't packed anything, but all my clothes are folded and put away neatly so I just have to throw them in the suitcase. Any of the mementos I brought when I moved in are still sitting in a box in the living room. I just never got around to making Brian's home my home. It makes this easier.

Mama Stratford and I talked about my plans when she came by yesterday. It was harder to tell her goodbye than I thought it would be. Kathryn is one of those women who weaves her way into the fabric of your very being, and it felt like ripping myself away from a beloved friend when I told her I will never forget how amazing she is. I hope when Brian finds his girl she knows just how lucky she is to be part of this family. I wish I could be part of it longer.

Dear Britton,

I leave tomorrow. Tonight, you're beside me, curled up on the bed sleeping soundly. You'll never know it's missing, but I'm taking the little knitted cap Grandma Kathryn made you. It smells like you. It's the only thing I'll take.

I love you. I will always love you.

Love,
Emily

Chapter 22

Emily
Departure

Brian gently shakes my shoulder to wake me and I'm gripped with fear he knows my plans to leave. Immediately, I'm defensive and it comes off as mean. The guilt eats away as he apologizes for waking me.

"Dad called. Something is wrong with the hot water heater at the house and he needs me to come over," he says. Tucking his T-shirt into his jeans, I take in his features — the way his hair is disheveled, how he's scruffy from being pulled in too many directions to take the time to shave, that his boots are on but not tied. I want to be in love with him. I want to tell him I won't be here when he gets back. I want to say goodbye. "If you need anything, call me. If I don't answer, call the house. Mama should be there."

He kisses me on the cheek. It's apologetic and platonic. It's my child's father hoping I'll be okay for a few hours while he's gone. It's Brian being Brian, forever a gentleman even though he could have just as easily turned it off and told me how horrible I was being. He walks out of the bedroom, and a few minutes later I hear the door open and then quietly close.

I breathe in deeply. And then I roll over and bury my face in his pillow so I don't wake the baby while I sob uncontrollably.

This is the hardest day of my life.

~*~*~*~

"Mama? You'll be there when I get there, right?" My voice hitches. I swallow back the emotions. I need to keep it together for just a couple more hours.

"I will. Are you sure about this?"

"It's the only choice. It's about seven hours between here and Biloxi, so I should be able to make it in one shot. I'll let you know when I've gotten to my mom's, but after that I don't know how often I'll contact you. It's going to hurt too much."

"I know, sweetheart," she says, then I hear the scratching sound of the mouthpiece being covered. In the background I can hear Tommy asking a question. He's going to hate me as much as his brother will. Everything in me aches right now. Mama comes back on the line and says, "It'll all be alright. I'll be here, you just get here when you get here."

I gather the clothes Britton might need throughout the day, plus extras, and pack them into a small suitcase. I put in a full pack of tiny diapers and extra wipes. He cries out from the crib in his room as I'm mixing bottles and loading the diaper bag. He's staring at the mobile above him when I walk back into his room and I love him so deeply in this moment that I take more pictures just so I never forget how I feel right now.

The bags are by the door. All of them. I never planned to take everything I brought when I moved in, so I have two suitcases of my clothes and the box of stuff from the living room. That's it.

"Are you ready, little man?" I ask as I clip him into his carseat and tighten the straps. I make sure the spare base for the carrier is on the counter along with the papers from the attorney granting Brian full custody. I still don't know how John made it happen. I didn't ask. The last time I met with him, we went over my will one last time and I made Mama beneficiary on the trust for Britton. She knows. I know she'll see everything is taken care of. "Grandma Kathryn is waiting for you. She's going to make everything okay and help you and Daddy adjust."

I load the car quickly and try not to draw attention to myself as I move out of the apartment. It's Saturday and it's still early, just a little past eight in the morning.

The world is trying to wake up.

I'm trying to run away.

The drive to Mama and Ben's takes an eternity, but as the house comes into view I'm washed in a calm I haven't felt in months.

"Someday when you have a new mom, I hope you'll know how much I love her for choosing you," I say. "You and Daddy are a package deal."

Brian will choose the perfect girl to take care of our son forever, but she's going to have the bigger responsibility of choosing both of them. His entire world for the last three weeks has revolved around Britton, and that's the way it always will be. When Brian finds her and they add to the family we've already started, the love Brian has now will only grow exponentially. I've accepted that my role here was to give him this gift. He might not see it when I turn around and walk back out that door, but I have a hard time believing everything that has happened to get us to this point is for nothing.

I park the car, but leave it running. It's cold out even for the beginning of February, and I shiver as I walk around the car to pull Britt, his suitcase, and the diaper bag from the backseat. I do my best to carry it all to the house without anyone seeing me, but I should have known better. The back door opens and Tommy walks onto the deck. He stands silently for a moment with a cup of coffee watching the sun rise higher behind a barn on the property. He doesn't see me until I'm almost to the stairs, and then — "Em? What are you doing here?"

He sets his cup down and rushes to the bottom of the stairs. He kisses my cheek and then smiles broadly at me. Taking the bags from me, he heads toward the house.

"Brian didn't say you were coming over. I'll let him know you're here," he says. I don't have a chance to tell him not to before we walk into the kitchen.

Mama stands at the counter peeling apples and when I come in she stops, lifts her eyes upward, takes a deep breath, and then releases it before wiping her hands on the dishtowel hanging on the stove. Her eyes tell me more than her mouth will say while anyone else is within earshot. Tommy sets the bags down and, though he eyes the little suitcase curiously, says nothing as he heads toward the basement door.

I mouth the words, "I'm sorry," as Mama walks toward me.

"Hush now. No apologizing, we've already done that." I'm dying inside even more than I already was. "He's going to want answers. If you don't want him coming to find you, you need to make it good."

"I'll break him if I'm mean. I've been acting mean for weeks and I hate it. This isn't me."

"We know. He knows. He'll be too busy to break for a while. I'm more afraid what you say will hurt you more than anything because it won't be the truth, but it'll be enough to make him stop while you go," she says just loud enough for me to hear. Kneeling down, she loosens the straps on Britt's seat and makes quick work of unbuckling him. "Come see Grandma Kathryn for just a minute and then your mama needs to love on you."

She takes a long look at him and hands him to me. She watches me touch his fingers and kiss his head, breathing in his new baby smell. I watch her heart break for me as I silently say goodbye to my only child, as I whisper to him that he will always feel my love no matter where he is, that I'll watch over him.

The first tears fall into his fluffy newborn hair, and I hear Brian and Tommy talking as they come up the stairs from the basement.

"Why would she bring a suitcase?" Tommy asks.

"Extra clothes for the baby probably," Brian says as he reaches the doorway. He sees me standing in the middle of the kitchen, my face tear-streaked, and he stops in his tracks. His eyebrows knit together as he watches me, trying to make sense of what's unfolding before him. "Emily, what's the matter?"

"I can't," I say, but then I stop. I swallow the lump in my throat, kiss Britton one last time, and hand him to Mama. I'm going to break us. "I can't do it, Brian. It's too much."

"What's too much?" The fear, it's so strong it radiates off him. I know he's been worried about me. He's asked me time and again if I want to talk to someone about depression. He has no idea. "The baby? We can ... we can get a nanny to help."

He's trying to problem solve and I don't want him to. I shake my head. "No. I just, I can't do this."

He steps closer to me, and I step away. I look at Mama and she turns to walk to the other room with the baby so neither of them hear when I break apart our family.

"What can't you do?" His voice rises and I hear the anger he's been holding back for weeks. "'This' is pretty broad, Emily."

He takes another step toward me and I freeze.

"I can't be his mom. I can't play house with you. I can't love you. I can't do this!" I yell at him as tears stream down my face because every single thing I threw at him was a lie. I take one more deep breath and I bury the knife I've already shoved into his heart. "He's yours. I never wanted to be a mom."

His face is ashen. I can't find the strength to say more, nor do I need to. He got the message. He looks grief-stricken as I cover my mouth, turn away from him, and walk out the door.

He doesn't follow me.

I don't look back.

"What the hell is the matter with you?" Tommy's voice bellows behind me as I reach the car.

"Tommy, don't." I turn to face him.

"The hell you never wanted to be a mom. You're so full of shit," he says, angrily. "You need to tell me what's going on because I don't believe for one minute you don't love that child to the ends of this earth."

"Tommy, please. I can't—"

"I keep hearing this phrase, 'I can't.' What exactly is it you can't do, Em?"

"I can't," I choke on the words. "I can't let him watch me leave. I have to go. Please, Tommy. I have to go. There's something I have to do and I can't be a mom and do that, too."

I plead with him as I open the car door. I beg him to leave me alone, just let me go. But he won't.

"I know Brian's been worried, I've been worried, but I don't think you'd do anything to hurt yourself. You're stronger than that. So, fine, I'll let you go," he says, walking closer. He puts his face right in front of mine. He's close enough I can feel the warmth coming off him. He's close enough I can see all the worry in his eyes. He's close enough to hug, but if I did that I wouldn't ever leave. "But, you call me when you get to where you're going, Emily, because whatever is going on is bigger than you can handle on your own and I'm not letting you do it alone. You call me, or, God willing, I will come find you."

I let him have the last word. I slide into the running car and back down the driveway, leaving Tommy standing in the yard. He reaches his hand up as if he's going to wave to me, but then places it behind his head, pulls his ball cap off, and watches me leave. When I reach the road, he's turned around and is walking to the house.

I make as few stops along the way as I can, but it's dark when I pull into the driveway at my mom's house several hours later. Mississippi. Home. I didn't think I would come back to die, but here I am. I kill the engine and sit staring at the house I grew up in. Nothing here has changed since I left, at least not on the outside. Inside, though, the heartache has grown. It will only get worse with time before she grows weary from it and lets go.

"This isn't how I wanted it to end, you know?" I say, looking up through the open window at my mother. She came out of the house and silently stood waiting for me to acknowledge her. The grief she's already suffered has aged her since I was here a few months ago. "I never thought this is how it would be. Didn't I pay my debts?"

Opening the door, she kneels down and reaches in to unbuckle me as though I am a child who lacks the skills to do it myself. I don't tell her, "don't."

I'm tired. I let her do this one thing because we both need her to take control of this; I can't.

"What debts?" Her eyes connect with mine, aghast at the notion I might believe this is my fault. "Emily, this isn't anything you caused. We're going to fight it just like we did before."

"But we won't win."

"We'll try. As long as you want to, we'll try."

~*~*~*~

Mom gets me into the house and settled into my old bedroom. I finally take the time to eat before falling into bed. Sleep doesn't come easily ...

Dear Britton,

This morning, I left you. I was planning to get up early and be gone before your dad had a chance to wake for the day. Instead, Grandpa Ben called and needed him to come to the house. It was almost easier that way. It gave me a few more hours with you while I packed and I'm blessed to have had those extra moments with you.

His face when I told him, "I can't do this," was a mix of horror and fear and anger, but he never uttered an unkind word. The sadness in his eyes reflected the sadness in my heart.

I made memories of his love for you that I will have forever. Memories of his kindness. Of all the good he's given me. Even in our worst moments, he was graceful in the way he treated me.

The only problem is, he thinks I left because I can't handle parenthood. We've had the conversations about how tired I am. We've talked about how much of a struggle it is for me to get out of bed. He's brought up time and again how he thinks I should talk to my doctor about my feelings. We've had all those conversations and, somehow, it's easier to pretend those things are the problems I'm dealing with. Some might say postpartum depression is easier to cope with than cancer. Take a pill or two and you'll feel better. Depression isn't terminal. It's easier to lie about being depressed than staring your expiration date in the face. Or maybe they're both a death sentence.

I second guessed myself every mile farther away from you I traveled. While I still second guess, I know this is what I need to do. You're in the best hands and the most capable arms of an absolutely amazing father. I pray some day when you're older you can forgive me for leaving you. I pray someday, when your dad finds the girl of his dreams, she's able to be all the mommy to you I was unable to be.

Someday, if you read these letters, I hope you'll know I did the best I could.

Love,
Emily

Chapter 23

Tommy

Brian and I went back to his apartment and he found everything still there, except her clothes and anything of sentimental value to her.

"She's been planning this," he says, looking at an envelope on the counter.

"What makes you say that?" I look over his shoulder and see the return address for a local attorney.

"She terminated her rights to him, Tommy. Why would she do that? I know it was hard getting used to being a parent. It's been hard on me, too, but it's parenting. It's not supposed to be easy."

I don't have an answer for my brother, but I'll try to get one. "Right now, I think the most important thing to figure out is how you're doing it on your own."

He's quiet as he reads over the documents. When he's done, he folds them, and places them back in the envelope. I'm certain he's in shock from it all. We're all in shock. I caught Mama crying in the rocking chair with Britt when I went back in the house. Dad came up from the basement and was giving Brian the third-degree trying to find out what happened and why he wasn't going after her. Brian just looked defeated. He still does and it's been hours since she left.

The last few weeks I've seen Emily look absolutely blissful and totally destroyed. It's frightening to watch someone you care about sway from one end to the other of the emotional spectrum and not know a damn thing about making it better for them. When Brian went back to work a week after Britt was born, I made sure to stop in whenever I could. It took work to get her to smile any time I was with her over the last several days, but at least I made sure she was eating.

"What are you going to do, Bri?"

I look at my brother and all he can do is shake his head.

"I don't know. I have no idea how to raise a kid, and now I have to do it on my own."

I remind him he won't be doing it alone. He says he needs to figure out daycare. I tell him to break his lease. He tells me to move in.

"That won't solve your babysitter problem if I'm working, too," I say. "Brian, move back home. Mama and Dad have enough room for all of us."

He promises to think about it. I give it a few days before he's calling Mama for help.

Before we go back to the homestead, he tries to call Emily.

She doesn't answer.

He leaves a message.

It's a long rambling apology. He never says a cross word. He tells her she can come home.

Brian is devastated, but not for himself. For Britt.

"I didn't think she would answer, but I had to try," he says.

~*~*~*~

Promises are promises. I called and kept on calling her until she finally picked up three days later. The last message I left was a threat to call her mama and find her that way, so I think that's what did it.

"Jesus, Tommy, quit." That's how she answers the phone when the call finally connects.

"Really? That's how you talk to me after what you pulled? You got some explaining to do, Emily."

The line is quiet and I think maybe the call was dropped, so I pull my phone away from my ear and see that, nope, we're still connected.

"Why do you need to know so badly?"

Her voice sounds a million miles away and I question why I'm so adamant.

"Because he's my nephew and someday he's going to have questions. Someone needs to be able to answer them."

And then I hear words I never in a million years thought I would hear from her.

"I have cancer, Tommy."

Then there's silence from both of us. I wait for the punchline. There isn't one.

"That isn't funny, Em."

"I didn't think it was funny either when I found out, but it is what it is."

"How long have you known?"

"For certain? I was thirty-six weeks pregnant. They suspected it was back a few weeks before that, though," she says.

"Back? As in you went through this before?"

"When I was a kid," she says, but her voice sounds so stiff and rehearsed. It's as though she practiced how to tell me and made it robotic enough to remove any emotion from the conversation. "Tommy, I don't want to do this. It's been too much this week."

Robot or not, I hear her voice start to crack a little.

"You can't tell Brian."

"Doesn't he have a right to know?"

"No. Yes. Eventually? Eventually he'll know, but not right now. Tommy, promise me you won't tell him. I don't want him worrying about me. I don't want ..." her voice trails off, but I can fill in the blanks.

"You don't want him to feel guilty for being mad?"

She takes a deep, strangled breath on the other end of the line. Her voice fills with unshed tears as she attempts to keep the emotion from capsizing her willingness to stay strong.

"I want him to enjoy raising our baby. I expect he's going to be mad for a long time because of how I handled it. He would have come after me if I hadn't done it this way."

Bet your ass he would have, is what I'd like to say to her. Instead, I hold my tongue and curse under my breath. "Where did you go?"

"Biloxi. I'm with my mom and the doctor who treated me when I had Leukemia before. I'm in good hands, Tommy. You don't need to worry."

But I will worry, and that's when I tell her if I have to promise not to tell my brother she has to promise to let me come see her. I'm the only connection Britt will have to her when he's older and I don't want him to miss out on his mom. Regardless of how Brian feels now, when we're all a little older and we can all think a little clearer, we're going to want to have this connection with Emily. Won't we?

Emily finally breaks down and gives me her mom's address. Before we get off the phone, I've already made mental notes of when I can make the drive to see her. I don't care that she says she's in good hands. I need to see for myself. I don't think she'll ever know how much she's done for me in the short time she's been my friend, but I'll do everything in my power to repay the kindness until I can't anymore.

Chapter 24

Emily

I started my first cycle of chemo two weeks after I got back to Mississippi. It's just as horrible as I remember.

We'll try. I promised Mom we'd try.

"He's beautiful, Emmy," Mom says looking through a stack of pictures that arrived today. "I wish you'd let me come see him before you left."

I hear myself tell her she would have tried to convince me to stay there. She doesn't deny it.

She pulls a picture of Brian and Britton from the top of the pile. I snuck a picture of the two of them after a long, sleepless night when Brian fell asleep on the couch with the baby curled up in the crook of his arm. There's no denying Britton is a Stratford, and I smile the first real smile I've been able to muster in weeks.

"Did you love him? Brian, I mean."

"I wanted to. I made myself find reasons not to. When I found out it was back, it was easier to keep my heart locked up, Mom."

"And the baby?"

"I'll never stop loving him."

Dear Britton,

You are six weeks old. I can hardly believe it's been three weeks since I held you, since I smelled your tiny head and kissed your itty-bitty hands. My heart aches, but I know now I made the right decision. My body is weak.

I met with my oncologist and the news is as I expected. We'll try treatment, but the chances of it saving me are slim. It's more likely that my life will be prolonged, but with what quality? I'll try it. We'll see what happens.

I love you forever.

Love,
Emily

Chapter 25

Emily

End of Chemo: First Course

I'm shocked when Mom walks into my room and announces I have a visitor.

"Told you I would call your mama and come find you," he says from the doorway.

"Oh, my Lord, it's the one and only Thomas Stratford. What are you doing in Biloxi?"

I'm finishing up the first course of chemo and it's been brutal. I feel worse than I did when I was just letting the cancer do its thing. If trying to survive hurts this much, why the hell am I doing it?

"Hey sweet girl," he says, twisting his hat in his hand. "I just couldn't keep myself away any longer."

My mom notices his fidgeting and places her hand on his arm before excusing herself.

"Liar."

"Ouch. That wasn't nice," he says. Smiling at me, he steps further into the room. My bubblegum pink bedroom. Mom never painted it after I left for college. "This is ... very pink."

I laugh, but it's cut short and he winces along with me.

"Actually, I have a friend from college that lives nearby. I might have told a little white lie to the family about coming to visit him. I'll get together with him, but I came to see you," he says. His eyes turn serious as he says, "I figure I can give your mama a break for a bit. It'll give us a few days to paint each other's nails and watch lame rom-coms. Plus, I can give you a proper update on things back home."

I reach up and touch the scarf I've carefully tied around my head. He sees it. It's just a nervous habit at this point to touch it. It feels like everyone looks at it and, if they don't know, they want to ask.

"I shaved it off pretty early on."

"You know I don't care about your hair. It's just hair, Em."

"No. It's not." It's evidence of the damage being done inside me. It shows off my failure to stay healthy. All the pretty scarves in the world won't make that go away.

"It can grow back."

I nod because I don't want to explain to him why it isn't just hair. He understands without me saying anything at all. Tommy always seems to understand. He lays down on my bed with me and I listen intently as he tells me all the things I've missed. He does it in a way, though, that makes me feel like I haven't missed much at all.

Dear Britton,

Uncle Tommy came to visit me. It's been a long six months since I last saw you and his trip to Mississippi was a bright spot in a dark place for me. He brought me pictures and told me all the things you're doing, like sitting up by yourself and trying new foods. He said you're really enjoying squash and applesauce. I imagine Thanksgiving and Christmas will be your favorite holidays when you're a bigger boy.

I know by the time you're old enough to read these letters memories like the first foods you tried may seem like silly things for me to be excited about, but I've heard it's normal for first time parents to want to burn all the "firsts" into their brains. I'd like to think if I was still with you, I'd be relishing all these tiny moments. Maybe your dad is doing just that and trying to make up for my absence. Maybe he's taking pictures of you trying all these new activities, like the other day when he took you to the playground and you went down the slide with Grandpa Ben for the first time. I hope he is. I want him to document every second he can so if he thinks he's missed something he can go back and watch you grow up all over again.

Someday when you're big he'll want to go back and remember all those little things. I hope you will sit with him and look at pictures from when you were tiny, spend time with him and laugh about the silly things he kept track of. You only have so many chances to build meaningful relationships with people. Take those chances, especially with your daddy. You're his whole world.

Love,
Emily

Chapter 26

Emily
Britton: One Year Old

A year. An entire year has passed. I'm in my second course of treatment. The first wasn't enough.

The second won't be either.

Mom and I went on an adventure to a local bakery yesterday where I picked out a small cake. We had it decorated with "Happy 1st Birthday" scrawled across the top.

"Are you going to blow out the candle?" she asks.

Maybe this was a bad idea. I just wanted to feel ... something. I wanted to celebrate that first birthday with him.

My phone beeps and I look. A text message from Tommy with a picture of Britton covered in frosting. I smile and blow out the candle.

Dear Britton,

It's hard to believe an entire year has passed. You're getting so big and handsome. Uncle Tommy sent me a picture of you with your cake, or what was left of it after you smashed it apart. I laughed until I cried.

You've had an amazing first year and learned so many new things. I get to watch from a distance, but I'm glad I'm letting you do all of it without me. Daddy's doing such a wonderful job. I knew he would. He's a strong man. You come from a family of beautiful and loving individuals. I couldn't have asked for a better father for you. Maybe it was destiny. Maybe fate played a hand.

God knew what we all needed. He delivered.

Love,
Emily

Chapter 27

Emily
Britton: Eighteen Months Old

"Emmy? Can I ask you something?" Mom asks as she pulls a chair up beside my bed.

It's been a rough few weeks. We're taking a break before deciding if I want to try another course of chemo. I feel like nothing will work. We can either burn all of my insides and pray for the best or I could just stop and wait for it to take me.

Waiting might feel better.

The end result will be the same.

I put my book down and look at my mother. She's going to ask me something hard. I can see it in her eyes.

"Will I ever get to meet him?" I notice the pictures in her hand. They're new ones Tommy brought on his last trip. Britton is eighteen months old and such a busy little boy. He's been keeping Kathryn and Ben on their toes while Brian is at work. "I just ... I wonder about him. You're my only child. He's my only grandchild."

We've never had this conversation before. She always seems happy with the information we do get since I'm not supposed to know anything at all.

"Mom, I —" I stop and collect my thoughts. "I don't think it would be right to interfere now. Just let him grow up."

"I'll never get to know my grandson. You're making me promise you that?"

"I am," I say, but not without hesitation. I gave up my rights, but does it extend to her? I never asked that. I never even thought about it. I selfishly made decisions.

"But why?"

"I don't know."

Dear Britton,

Grandma Long asked me today if she'll ever get to meet you. I didn't know what to tell her. Part of me wants her to come see you after I'm gone, but I don't know how your dad might feel about that. Right now, you're both comfortable living with Grandma Kathryn and Grandpa, and I just don't want to mess that up. I've already screwed up so many things. I don't know what the best decision is anymore.

Love,
Emily

Chapter 28

Emily
The End

"She's not doing well at all. You might want to make plans to come soon. ... There's a nurse coming in the morning," she says quietly into the phone. "You can stay here if you'd like. I know it's short notice."

It's March 31. I didn't think I'd make it to March at all.

I catch a glimpse of my mom as she paces the short hallway outside my bedroom. There's only one person she would call and tell to come soon. Tommy will probably be here by tomorrow.

Mom ends the call and I watch as she buries her face in her hands. She's aged in the two years I've been home and I hate that it's taken so long for me to leave. Did I really need to be here this much longer? A year would have been long enough. But this has been more than I bargained for. Two years of putting her through watching me try to get better. Two years of Tommy making trips to see me and leaving defeated when I'm dying anyway. Two years of watching my son grow up in pictures.

At least I have pictures.

She notices I'm awake and I watch as my mother, devastated and beyond repair, paints on a smile for my benefit.

"Hey, sweetie, I didn't realize you were awake. Do you want to try some soup?"

I shake my head a little. "No, thank you. I could use some water, though."

She nods, smiles again, and leaves the room.

I feel the notepad beneath my fingers. I'm still gripping the pen from when I drifted off earlier. I need to finish this. I need to send these letters home with him. I need them all to know how much I love them even when I'm no longer around to tell them.

~*~*~*~

My room is still swathed in darkness when the clicking of the desk lamp wakes me. The soft glow washes over him as it comes to life and for a moment I wonder if I've left in my sleep. I've heard someone familiar is the one who comes to lead you home, but my angel looks just like Tommy. I'm relieved and saddened to know I'm still here when he moves to the bed and bends to kiss my forehead.

"Nope. I'm still alive after all," I rasp, my throat dry from sleep.

He chuckles. "So far, yeah. Why do you say that?"

"You looked like someone who came from heaven, that's all."

"Well, now. It's not everyday I get likened to a celestial being so I'll take it as a compliment," he says. Smiling down at me, he kneels beside the bed. "Sorry I woke you. I didn't realize how bright the lamp is."

There's too much sadness in his eyes. I don't want him to feel this way.

"What can I do to make it better?" he whispers.

"You're already doing it."

Sleepily, I reach for the hair brush on the bedside table. He picks it up for me but doesn't place it in my open hand. Helping me sit up, Tommy gently sits on the bed with me and begins pulling the bristles through my hair. It's grown back quickly and just barely touches below my ears, but it'll never be long again. I lean against him, exhausted from the effort sitting up requires.

"I finished the letters."

I feel his chest stop moving as he holds his breath.

"All of them?"

"All of them." He doesn't know I started writing Britton letters before he was born. There's a large envelope with all of the notes inside it, each of the ones for special people and occasions sealed separately.

Tommy's arms wrap around me and I lay my head against him. He's the best friend I could have asked for through all of this. We both know it's coming to an end. "I'm so tired. I just want to go home already."

His chest quakes beneath me as he holds onto time, memories, and all his promises.

Chapter 29

Tommy

It's unseasonably warm for the end of April, but still smells like those first glorious days of spring — fresh tilled dirt from the neighboring farms and gardenias.

I'm not ready for this to happen. I just saw her a couple weeks ago and now she's gone.

Emily's mom called me around five this morning, but I was already awake. I knew she had a difficult day yesterday and I just couldn't manage to sleep. I swear I heard Emily call my name as I stood at Mama's kitchen sink sipping a cup of coffee and looking out over the back field. I felt her leave on a strong gust of wind as it rushed through the open window and I just stood there.

That's where Mama finds me still a little while later. Here I am, a grown man, standing at the open window with tears streaking my face. She turns me to face her and holds my chin in the palm of her hand. Mama has always been really good at keeping secrets — that's probably where I get it from — and when she sees my face she knows something major has happened. It isn't something I can keep to myself. The grief is too much to carry alone.

"She was my best friend, Mama, and I couldn't talk to you or Brian about what she was going through. I promised her I wouldn't, not until it was time," I say, another swell of tears breaching the dam and tracing their way down my face.

"Who, Tommy?" she asks, her face scrunching in concern.

"Emily. Emily died this morning, Mama." Her face falls, but she doesn't look surprised. Just sad, so very sad. The words push through my lips. "She didn't leave because she didn't love Britt, Mama. She had cancer and went home to Biloxi for treatment."

"I know, baby. I know she did." And I wonder if I heard her right.

She pulls me to her and shushes me. I swallow down what I can of my emotions. I have to, because there's a chance I could wake Brian and Britt and I know now is not the time for me to tell them. Emily's letters were written to be given when they were ready.

"Mama, you can't tell Brian," I say quietly into her shoulder. I stand tall and silently plead with her. "Please? There are letters and I have to wait to give them."

"How long do you have to wait? That's a huge responsibility."

"The first one for Brian is for his wedding day," I say, and I know it sounds crazy. Brian isn't even dating and hasn't since Em left. "I don't know how I'm going to do this."

Mama smiles at me. "Thomas, you and Emily were obviously pushed together for a reason. Coincidences don't exist. You'll do it, and you'll do it honorably. She wouldn't have picked you if she thought you couldn't handle the job."

I take what she's said to heart and tamp down the grief attempting to billow out of me as we settle ourselves at the table for another cup of coffee. I take in the gloriousness of the sunrise and share stories with Mama from the trips I made to Mississippi to visit Emily. I have a friend from college living near Emily and her mama, so I never actually lied about going to see him.

Catching myself chewing on my thumb, I drop my hand back to my lap and rest the other on the table beside my mug. What if I'm making the wrong decision withholding this information from Brian? We've worked so hard to get back to normal the last couple years. The last thing I want is to mess it up by keeping my promise to Emily.

Mama reaches across the wooden surface and gently grasps my fingers. "You know, your brother will understand. When the time comes, he'll see why you didn't tell him you kept in touch with her and he'll come to terms with why she left. Keep your word, Tommy."

And with that, I nod my head and I excuse myself to hide away in my room. I find myself crouching beside the bed as I carefully open the envelope with my name scrawled across the front of it in her tired penmanship and my heart begins to ache. That's when it hits that she's truly gone and I cry like a baby while I read the letter that's been sitting in my dresser since the last time I saw Emily.

Dear Tommy,

Take a deep breath. I know why you're reading this. I told you to wait until it was time, and if you've broken the seal on that giant envelope I sent home with you after your last visit then my mom must have called you. I'm so sorry …

If I left before you were ready for me to go, please put it on your heart to forgive me for not allowing you closure. I don't think that has happened though. We've always found closure no matter the circumstances or conversation. And if you didn't find closure, I hope these letters will help you. There are a lot. I've been busy, but I've gotten tired. Dying kind of takes it out of you.

Dying is a funny thing, you know? Maybe not to other people, but right now, to me, it's funny. I've tried to be a good person and kind, and now? Now I have trouble doing anything for myself. I've come face-to-face with my mortality and accepted my death as imminent, but truly feel God has a funny way of thanking me for my service all these years by giving me the boot out of the physical world right when my life could begin. I was able to be a mom, and then I made the choice to sacrifice myself for my son. I'll never regret that decision, though. I just wish, maybe, the dying part wasn't taking so damn long. I thought the treatments alone would kill me. I didn't expect to make it past Britton's first birthday and now we're closing in on his second. But here I am, finally standing a little bit closer to death's door.

I failed to take the time to tell you how much you have meant to me over the last couple of years. My body has been ready for a while now, but my heart has had trouble letting go. I think the reason He kept me around so long was because of you. I wasn't needed for Britton, but I was a requirement for you as you were for me. You'll never know all the things you taught me, and after this I'll never be able to tell you. Please know that every lesson you gave me, even if it wasn't meant to be a lesson, and every time you helped me it was another reason for me to believe there is something out there greater than I. There was no coincidence in my meeting Brian, or Britton being conceived, or you being at the apartment the day I received that phone call.

So now I'm left wondering, how do you say goodbye to your best friend? How do you say that final "See you later" to the one person who wouldn't let you push them away? Thank you, Tommy, for not letting me push you away when I left Tennessee. You are my only connection to Britton, and you have brought so much joy to my life not only by sharing him with me, but also by simply being yourself when you've come to visit. You remind me so much of your brother, yet the two of you are so different, and I love you a tremendous amount for those differences.

Love is tricky, though. There are so many kinds of it out there that sometimes it's difficult to distinguish which one you're feeling for another person. There were times when I know you and I questioned our love for each other. I think, had life turned out differently, that love would have always remained platonic. Not because it couldn't have been more, but because I wasn't your one. You'd said time and again that you felt Brian could have fallen in love with me, the romantic kind, but I can say with certainty I wasn't his one either. I'm relieved, because you're both going to find the women who will make your life complete — the ones you will build homes and raise families with. You'll both know as soon as the pieces slide into place who she is. You're going to find her. You just have to stop searching so damn hard.

The thing about looking for love is, it's not something you can seek and find. It has to be created and nurtured. Like the perfect storm, you need all the right conditions and the right person for it to be love. Stop trying to create the conditions you think will make it easier for someone to fall in love with you. Love happens when you aren't looking for it.

When she comes along, she's going to be perfect. I hope you know that. You just have to seize the opportunity to actually believe it.

Now, for some instructions about those other letters. I've labeled them all, obviously, and sealed them because I don't want you reading them before you give them out. Don't be nosy. Especially with the one addressed to the Future Mrs. T. Stratford. That one isn't for you either. There's nothing crazy in there, or any of them for that matter. The most important letters, though, are for Britton. I'll leave it up to Brian when to give them to him, but there are some that I hope will be given to him at certain times. The day he gets his driver's license. The day he graduates from high school. The day he leaves for college. His first heartache. The day he marries his one. The birth of his first child.

I told you ... I've been busy. I tried to cover all the big milestones and, while Brian doesn't have to honor my wishes, I've said a little prayer that he will. Once he reads his letter, he'll be more open and understanding.

Love,
Em

P.S.: If Brian doesn't marry a girl named Stella, trash that letter.

Chapter 30

Tommy
Four years later

Emily died a few months after Britt's second birthday, after fighting the cancer. She fought hard, but it was more than her body could handle. The last time I saw her, she was so thin and frail. I held her hand and cried because, while I spent month after month watching my brother struggle with what he thought was the truth, I knew the truth. Brian thought she simply couldn't love Britt, or him, enough to make it work.

It's my job to tell him how wrong he has been.

It eats away at me every time I think about it. Over the years, every time I've opened the letter she left me, I've wondered how much longer it would be before I was supposed to give Brian the stack of envelopes she handed over the day I left her dying in her bubblegum pink bedroom in Mississippi.

Tomorrow my brother gets married to the woman of his dreams. My nephew accepted her into his heart and life. No questions asked. Stella has been the mom to Britt that Emily prayed he would someday have, the mom she prayed Brian would give to him. If I'm being totally honest, I think Emily prayed for Stella, too, because she left a letter specifically for her. How she knew Brian would go home and marry his childhood sweetheart, I'll never know. I think Mama might know the answer to that, but she's not talking.

~*~*~*~

After searching for him at the cafe and at the house, I finally check the town park. I watch him for a few minutes, sitting on a swing in his tuxedo, while trying to build up the courage to talk to him until I finally take a deep breath and walk toward the swing set. I'm suddenly unsure if this is the right decision. Emily asked me to give him the letter when he found "her." She didn't specify when, though, and maybe their wedding day isn't the best time to do it. I'm already here, though, and despite what Emily might have meant, I feel this is when I'm supposed to do it. I can feel her everywhere.

"I checked the workshop. You weren't there. I went to the coffeehouse. Nada. Locked up tighter than a nun's habit," I say as he twists his neck to look at me. "But here? This is where you are on your wedding day?"

I grab the chains of the swing beside him and lift myself over and plop down into the seat. Once I'm settled, he tips the to-go cup in his hand and points at the gazebo across the lawn.

"That wedding Stell and I talked about back at Christmas? That's the gazebo it was in. I just wanted to come back here and remember how I felt watching her face that day," he says.

He pushes back in the swing and lets go, gliding through the crisp April air.

"And how do you feel?"

He doesn't hesitate. "Like she was the only other person in the world I wanted to spend forever with." I think a beat and push my swing back to catch up with him. "Today I'm finally going to get that."

It takes me a while, sitting on the swing set with my brother, before I can muster the courage to finally tell him. Up to this point, I was just enjoying being a kid. It's short lived, though, and I feel the crushing reality of my promises to Em bear down on me.

We bring our swings to a stop and I clear my throat, breaking the silence.

"I ... uh," I stumble. I clear my throat again and reach into my pocket. I catch his eye as I pull the white envelope from inside my tuxedo jacket. "I need to tell you something."

"If you tell me you can't stand up there with me, I will never forgive you, so it better be something like cancer," he says. I wince. He doesn't even know how close to the mark he is. "I can forgive cancer. Maybe." He shakes his head, laughs, and says, "No, I can't. What's up with the envelope?"

There is no easing into this conversation.

"Seriously, T, what's with the envelope?" he asks again, this time his voice wavers.

"It's from Emily."

There. I said it. And then he asks me what I mean, and I beg him to not be mad.

"It's a little late for that, don't you think?" He dropped his coffee cup and as I look at him, I see the red creeping up his neck. The anger of the past hitting him simply at the sound of her name. He reaches for the envelope, telling me to give it to him, but I pull away.

"Let me explain," I plead.

And for nearly an hour I talk about Emily. I talk about my trips to see her and the love she had for their son. I explain that she wasn't in love with Brian, just like he wasn't in love with her, and though they both already knew that, it's still torture to say that to my brother.

"She loved you because you gave her Britt, but she wasn't in love with you," I say. I leave out the part about her forcing herself to lock up the love she was growing for him because of her diagnosis.

He yells and screams, throwing in my face that she left. She couldn't handle it. The baby drained her. He wanted to tell her to just deal with it because that's what babies do.

"But instead of dealing with it, she left," he screams at me ... and I want to hate him for not being more understanding. He didn't see any of it. He didn't see she wasn't well. I know he's blamed it on baby blues and postpartum depression all these years. He can't see beyond the fact she left, though, to see the truth.

"She was sick, Brian!" I yell back. Then quietly, because it hurts like hell finally saying it out loud to him, I say, "She was sick. It wasn't just emotionally and mentally draining her to be a mom. Emily left you and started chemo a week later because she was afraid to let her son watch her die. She moved back to Mississippi with her mom to start treatment for leukemia."

He tells me I'm not making sense. She couldn't have been sick because he would have known. He says it more to himself than to me, and I see him trying to connect the dots from more than six years ago.

"How did I miss this?" He shakes his head as if trying to make sense of it all. So, I try to make sense of it for him.

"You were tired. You were working, trying to make a relationship work that wasn't meant to work. You were a new dad, and it was exhausting," I pause. I need to. I hate all of this. I hate that Emily kept it from him. I hate that Emily is gone. The last few years have just been ... hard. "More than that, though? She hid it from you."

It takes it all out of me to confess these truths to him, to share what I didn't know until after she'd already left. When I'm on the verge of tears I finally say, "She could have undergone treatment before Britt was born, but she didn't want to put him at risk."

I find the courage to unload all of my hurt, my pain of watching my best friend die and not being able to convince her to try one more round of chemo. I think the weight of it all finally hits home when he looks at me and I see my brother cry. He can't stop it from happening. "Why didn't she tell me? I could have helped her. I could have been there for her."

I wish he wouldn't try to make sense of it. She made the decisions she did because deep down she knew treatment wouldn't work. He needed to take care of Britton and he did that — he did exactly what Emily wanted him to do and Brian hated her for it because he had no idea why she left.

We sit silently, him contemplating what I've shared and me wanting to curl in a ball and forget April 22nd exists. I don't want to remember today and telling him this news; the last several moments could be stricken from history and I would be okay with that.

Then his anger comes back and Brian screams at me. He yells about me telling him about Emily's cancer. He snidely asks if she's going to show up today ... if she's going to try to make his wedding to Stella even more memorable. It kills me inside as I turn away from him and wipe the moisture from my face.

"No, Bri," I say, reaching over to grab his shoulder. He connects the dots when he looks at me again. I see it the second it clicks. I see when he realizes every reference to Emily I've made is past tense. I share with him the details about Emily's death, about the envelope filled with letters — one for him, one for Britton, and one for him and Stella. I don't share that Emily's one to Britt is probably more like one hundred, because she wanted to make sure he knew how much he meant to her. I don't tell him that I'm giving Stella her letter next. I pause a moment, caught off guard by the way he watches me as I speak as though he's not sure if I'm being honest. I trudge on. "It's everything she wanted to tell you and whomever you deemed worthy enough to be Britt's mom. Emily never told me exactly what the letters say, just that on the day you found *her* I was to give this to you."

I don't want to witness the moment he takes the papers from my hand, so I set my gaze toward the gazebo and silently pull the envelope from my jacket and pass it to him.

"I know things weren't always great for you guys when she was pregnant, but she was really trying to keep it together which I think also meant pushing you away so you wouldn't look for her after she left. She loved you so much simply because you gave her the chance to be a mom, even though she gave it all up. I think she knew you needed to have a purpose, too, and that purpose was my nephew."

He needs to absorb it all. He needs to read that letter. And I need to find a drink. It's been a really long, hard, four years.

Getting up from the swing, I grab the chain and pull it back as I walk away, leaving my brother alone with Emily's ghost.

Dear Brian,

This isn't meant to be some sort of Dear John letter, though I know when it reaches you that's likely how you will take it. I hope you read this to the end. I have a lot to say ... things I wish I said before I left but didn't take the time to.

The day I met you, I was smitten. I was getting over one heartache and had been dared by friends to spend Gavin and Shana's wedding weekend finding the perfect person to get over my failed relationship with. I planned to lose the bet because the last thing I really wanted to do was end up in the bathroom of a hotel room in tears because I'm bad at relationships. It's different for girls, you know. We don't just get over the heartache by climbing into bed with the first pretty smile we see. I'm sure you're seeing the irony in it considering our short history.

The truth is, I was just a woman you met at a wedding. I was just the friend of a friend you danced the night away with. I was just the person you fell into bed with that night.

It was one wonderful night.

That's all I was supposed to be for you. That's all you were supposed to be for me.

And then a month later I found myself asking Shana for your address. You were the man who danced into my life and then right back out and looking for you after that night was the last thing I ever planned to do. Then I found myself showing up on your doorstep with the first picture we had of Britton and fear. You'll never know the fear I felt. Without me telling you, you would never know I almost didn't tell you at all. I considered it, and then I considered how you would feel if years later you found out you had a child you had never met. I couldn't do that to you.

I never intended to get tangled up in you or your life. I wanted children, but I wanted to be in love before having a baby. This wasn't how I planned my life.

Plans change. It's as simple as that. I went from not even being sure I wanted to tell you, or that I wanted to raise a baby and thinking someone else could do it better, to praying every day that I would get to watch him take his first steps, say his first words, go to kindergarten, and someday raise a family of his own. I watched my belly grow, my skin stretch, and my body change. I welcomed it all.

I felt myself fall in love with you because of Britton and despite fate throwing us together in the most unlikely circumstances. I should have hated you for getting me pregnant, and at times I did, but it wasn't because I was pregnant. It had nothing to do with you at all. Strangers? A baby? How were we supposed to make that work? But you did. You made it work. How many books have been written that start like our life together did? Probably too many to count. The only difference was there wasn't going to be a "happily ever after." Not for me, anyway.

Of all the things to happen that I hadn't planned? My cancer coming back was the biggest one. I never thought it would happen. Not ever. I thought I'd beat it for good. I wanted so badly to not be a statistic. I prayed nightly to not have a recurrence. I wanted it to stay away so badly I never even told you I had beat it once before. I didn't want that to be part of our life together, so I deleted it from my history all together ... until it showed up again while I was pregnant with Britton. I made the decision to continue my pregnancy without treatment. It was up to me to wait no matter how many times the doctor told me I shouldn't. Our son was more important than me, and as long as I could keep him healthy until he was born, I was going to wait.

My oncologist thought I was reckless. I've never been reckless, but I was when I told her I needed a better option than putting my child at risk. So, we waited. I was living with Leukemia and refused to tell you because I didn't want you to be kind to me simply because I was sick. You were always kind. Even when we argued, you were nice about it. I didn't want to see you be sad and kind at the same time. Instead, I kept all the scared words I had to myself and only gave you my happy ones. That's what I tried to do. Did I succeed? For a while I thought I had, and then I started running out of happy words.

The day Britton was born, I made the best decision I could make for our family. I called my mom after you left the hospital and I started making a plan to leave. I took pictures — so many pictures — of our new baby, of you holding him, of your parents and Tommy holding him, of him sleeping next to you, and of him curled up in my lap after waking in the middle of the night. Every single photograph I took those first few weeks with him has eased the ache. I've asked to be buried with most of them because I felt so surrounded by love that I want to know what that feels like for eternity.

When I found out the cancer was back, Tommy was at our apartment. The doctor wanted me to come back in for additional testing and I fell apart. I couldn't tell him when he stood in our kitchen while I took the call. But he's a smart man, just like you, and knew just by looking at me something was wrong. He was relieved when I told him it wasn't the baby. Relieved until he realized the only other option was that there was something wrong with me. You all saw my health start to spiral downward, but he seemed to feel it right along with me. He wouldn't let it go, so once I left I told him every small detail of my years in remission.

And I begged him not to tell you. I begged him and pleaded with him.

Please, don't be angry with Tommy. He held my secret so you could focus on Britton, so you could hold our son instead of my hand as I was dying. I didn't want you to feel you had an obligation to me, of suffering with me through the pain and having to choose between our baby and being by my side. I couldn't ask you to make a choice like that. So, I made the choice for you; I chose our son for you.

I don't regret leaving. I regret making it easy for you to hate me because I left. I'm sorry. I'm sorry I made you hate me for leaving our son. I'm sorry you were left to raise him on your own. I'm sorry I couldn't have been healthy for him and you. I wonder every day what it would have been like to live and love you day in and day out. It weighed on me heavily for a while. Leaving was the best decision. If I left on good terms, though, there's no way you wouldn't have come looking for me, so I did the only thing I knew would keep you away. I found the mean girl I never could be as a teenager and let her loose. After holding so many emotions in for so long, unleashing that anger killed me. All the same, it wasn't as difficult as I thought it would be. I knew after that, you wouldn't come for me.

There were moments of clarity when I thought I should tell you, or when I felt like I should break Tommy free from our agreement. But I'd already been gone for a year and I couldn't try to walk back into your life. I couldn't call you up and say, "Hey Bri, remember me? By the way, I have Leukemia and I'm dying. Want to grab dinner?" I had already burned all my bridges.

If there had been a chance treatments would cure me instead of simply prolong my life, I might have considered staying. I might have tried harder. What would it have been like to stay forever? I knew the odds were against me. Call it intuition. Scientifically, I heard all the positives, all the ways I would bounce back and have quality instead of just quantity. This time, though, I knew it wasn't going to release me from its clutches. Cancer doesn't like to give up easily. I wasn't throwing in the towel when I left. I did fight. But I was losing. I stopped my treatment when we realized it wasn't working, that my cancer was more aggressive than we thought.

I felt better for a while and then it wasn't better. I found myself being sad and alone a lot more than I was comfortable with. I didn't want to be a person who feels comfortable surrounded by her own loneliness. That's part of why Tommy knew what was happening. He knew I needed him. We both needed a friend and found each other long before my diagnosis. He was a lost soul, what with his brother about to be a dad. He looks up to you so much and suddenly you were the one doing things backwards, so it was a difficult time for him. I hope he's had the chance to discover his purpose, because he does have one. He just needs a map. Be his guide.

Rather than focus on how horrible it is that I'm dying, I've set my sights on how much I loved, and lived, in such a short amount of time. I'm not even 30, but, God, I have been loved and given love so deeply. I was able to be a mom, and a daughter, and a lover, and a fighter ... and now? I'm tired, Brian, and I'm glad I made the decision to not make you endure this with me.

You're needed elsewhere.

Love,
Emily

Chapter 31

Tommy

Emily gave me the most difficult job. At some point during the course of our friendship, she learned about Stella and figured out a lot of stuff. I'm still not sure from where or how but, as always, I'd take a guess Mama was involved. We don't talk much about Em, but when we have I've always gotten the impression she knew more than either Brian or I were ever privy to.

"Why is there a letter for me? Brian and I weren't even together when she died. Tommy, he hadn't even moved back up here at that point," Stella says, the glow of pregnancy brightening her features.

I'm shoved momentarily back in time to Emily and how full of life she was at this stage. She was ready to do it all. Then it was torn away.

I take a deep breath, sighing deeply as though the air had been trapped for far too long. Finally, I find my words. "She knew someday Brian was going to do the fall in love and get married thing. Brian doing those things meant a woman in Britt's life, too. I think it's Emily's way of saying she trusts you to raise her baby, because she couldn't do it." Tears threaten to break through, and when I blink, they begin coursing down my cheeks. There's nothing I can do to make it better. I can't make it stop, so I just let them fall. "She might have made a poor choice not telling Brian what was going on, but in the end, she wanted nothing more than for him, for you, and for Britt to know you all have her blessing to love as a family."

Stella reaches up to wipe the tears from my face and whispers "thank you" in my ear as she pulls me to her. Stella holds onto me until I can't cry anymore and my tears dry up.

Before she lets me go, I whisper in her ear, "Take this, please. Read it. Please, know she would have loved you so much, Stell. She's the kind of woman you would have been friends with."

Dear Britton's Mom,

Believe it or not, I'm actually very okay with this. You are his mom, because if Brian is marrying you (or has already married you) he isn't doing it for himself and it wasn't a decision he made lightly.

Though I wasn't around long enough to see it for myself, Tommy keeps me updated on the boys as best he can. Brian hasn't focused on anything but our son since the day I left, so if he's taken the leap all the way to the altar, I'm sure it's because Britton and Brian both chose you to be in their lives.

You must be someone very special to have captured both their hearts and I can't tell you what an honor it is to have you raising Britton alongside Brian. He's a good man, and he needs a strong woman who can handle all the ups and downs of life and parenting. I know I don't know you, but Brian does, and his gut is usually pretty on point when it comes to trusting people.

When Brian and I were together, he had tons of pictures from his childhood scattered around the apartment. He loves the people in his life, past and present, and it always struck me as odd that after college he moved back to Tennessee instead of staying in New York where it seemed so many amazing memories were made in such a short amount of time. His heart was always up north. Occasionally, I would catch a glimpse of him looking at a photo of himself and Tommy sitting with a young girl. I asked him about it once. He got a wistful look in his eyes and smiled when he said her name, as if she hung the moon and lit the stars. I'm going to go out on a limb and say, if my instincts are right ... I hope he still looks at you like that, Stella.

Brian wouldn't speak an ill word about someone unless it was the truth, but right now, while I'm writing these letters, he doesn't know the truth. He knows what he believes to be the truth. What if he thinks that's enough? Has he painted me in a bad light? That's one thing I'm fearful about, but I would understand if he has. We didn't have a lot of time together before I walked away from them. I left. I'll never deny that. I can't deny it, because that's exactly what I did. I hate that I did it to them, but I didn't want to become a burden. The cancer treatments we've tried haven't worked. I didn't think they would. I'm terminal. I waited too long. If I hadn't waited and instead followed my doctor's advice to attempt to treat sooner, we might not have the son we do. He might not have been perfect like he is. I couldn't take that chance and I couldn't expect Brian to care for me while taking over full-time parenting when I was going through treatment. I promise you, though, I love that little boy with every fiber of my being. I love him so much I left so his daddy could focus solely on him. And in the time between then and now? He found you again. I think we all win in this one.

I'm more at ease with the thought of leaving this earth knowing Brian has found someone to love him and our little boy unconditionally.

As a mother, I hope you understand where my head and heart were when I made my decision. Out of all the choices I've had to make while fighting this disease, leaving him was the most difficult one. Tommy became my lifeline to Britton after I left. He's sent me videos and pictures. I have a few coloring pages, and they're my favorite pieces of art. It doesn't matter that they're just scribbles because our son colored them. It hurts less pulling away from the life I could have had with Britt when I was given the chance to see what an amazing child he was turning into.

Because of that, I'm okay with leaving. I'm ready to go.

Love,
Emily

Chapter 32

Tommy
Seven years after Emily's death
Britton: a few weeks shy of 9 years old

The thing about Emily is she wanted to be prepared for everything. How many people on their deathbed take the time to write letters to people who aren't even part of their lives yet? Em had a lot of opinions for me and about me. Mostly, she just wanted to make sure I lived up to my potential. She told me once that all she wanted was for me to shut up and be happy.

I am beyond happy. I got the girl. I got the perfect-for-us life. I'm about to be a dad. I finally stopped looking and when she found me ... there was a letter for her, too.

"Jace, before I forget, this is for you." I hand her the wrinkled envelope and watch her inspect the handwriting.

"You're giving me a letter written by another woman. How romantic of you," she says. She's teasing, but stops when her eyes scan up my legs to my face and she takes in my body language. My arms are crossed and I catch myself chewing on my thumb. She looks at me and the worry etches a few lines between her eyebrows. "Is everything all right?"

I want to tell her it isn't, but I truly have no idea. All I know is I was supposed to give my wife this letter on our first Christmas together.

"Tommy? You're scaring me."

"It's from Emily."

"Britt's mom Emily?" Her eyes drop to the envelope before meeting my gaze again. She's confused. "Why would you have a letter to me from Emily?"

I've told her about Emily. Jacelyn is one of the few people I've opened up to about my time with Em before she passed. Consequently, she's also aware of the letters Em wrote to all of us. I might have omitted the part where Emily had also written one for my future wife. For a woman who was dying, she certainly had a lot to say to all of us. During my last visit with her, she made sure I knew she needed me to get her words out there. She was compelled to talk to all of us even after she was gone.

I nod in response to Jacelyn's question. "Because she wrote them to all of us. Brian, Britt, Stella, me, and my wife. You're kind of my wife now. I mean, you have been for a while, but I was given explicit instructions as to when to give that to you," I say, gesturing to the paper in her hand with the thumb I'd been gnawing on.

Her eyebrow raises. "And those instructions said to give it to me at almost midnight on Christmas Eve?"

"Our first Christmas, but this is close enough. Are you going to open it?" I'm slowly dying inside wondering what Emily wrote to her.

"I'm a million days pregnant and exhausted from wrapping Britt, Emmy, and Jake's presents." I have nothing to offer but a blank stare. She's already past her due date. This is probably the last thing she needs right now, but she sighs and I know I've gotten my way. "Get out. She didn't write it for you, so I get to read it first. Alone. There's laundry downstairs that needs to be folded."

I smile and step toward her. My hands softly cup her face and she gives me a broad, but tired, smile. "I love you, Jacelyn Stratford. You are the best thing that has ever happened to me." I lean down and press my lips to hers, and she sighs just enough to open up for me to deepen the kiss. As I pull away, I press my forehead to hers and I whisper, "Best. Thing. Ever."

I turn to leave the room. I hear the crinkling of the paper as she carefully tears the envelope and pulls the letter from within. I close the bedroom door behind me and make my way toward the stairs, a smile crossing my lips as I think of all the ways Emily has influenced me since she left.

Dear Tommy's wife,

Mrs. Tommy? Mrs. T? I'm not sure how to address this one, so I hope I haven't already made it awkward. Knowing Tommy, the girl who captured his heart doesn't think this entire situation is strange at all. You're probably taking it in stride ... but if, by chance, you aren't and you think this is weird, maybe you should put this paper back in the envelope and hand it back to him.

I'm going to assume that didn't happen and you're still reading this, because Tommy doesn't make mistakes. I'm sure at some point Ben has told you that about his youngest son. He can screw some things up really bad, but in the end, he always makes the right choice.

He's a good man. Actually, he's amazing. When I first met Tommy, I was pretty sure he hadn't and would never grow up. He acted like a teenager, at best, most of the time and was struggling. He didn't know what he wanted to be when he grew up, but I know the last thing he really wanted to do was have to act like a grown up. Not all the time, anyway.

When I first met him, I was brand spanking new pregnant with Britton. All at once he acted like I had ruined his relationship with his brother and was giving him a new friend to play Legos with. I guess, in a way, both of those assumptions were correct. I didn't intentionally put a strain on his relationship with Brian, but I did take Brian away from him in the sense that he went from focused on his future to focused on our future overnight. I think Tommy got lost in the fray the first couple of weeks after I told Brian about the baby. It was very difficult for him and I hope there have been no lasting negative effects of that on their relationship. I would be devastated if I caused a rift in their brotherhood. Tommy and Brian have a bond unlike any I've seen before; they're about as close as twins can be without being twins. Tommy and I spent a lot of time talking about his feelings as my pregnancy progressed, so I feel like things were back to normal or as normal as they could be.

After watching him be an uncle, I can honestly say when Tommy becomes a father himself, if he hasn't already, those children will be the center of his whole entire world. I saw it every time he held Britton — the love and devotion he was giving his nephew was just a fraction of the emotion he will feel as a parent himself. And for a man, Tommy is pretty emotional. But if you've married him you know that. Being emotional isn't a bad thing and please remind him, if he ever starts to doubt how he's supposed to display his emotions, that the way he expresses himself is part of what makes you love him. There are times when he reeks of confidence, but beneath it all he might just be scared and ready to cry from nervousness or fear. Remind him when you have children that letting them see him cry is never a sign of weakness.

There were times during our discussions that Tommy left the room wiping his eyes, and I failed to tell him it's okay to cry. I know it wasn't my job to tell him, but I feel like I should have and I'm writing this now because I don't want to be too tired to say it before he comes back. I didn't want him to cry for me, but I'm blessed to know our friendship had as much of an impact on him as it did on me. I can say with all sincerity, Tommy was my best friend.

I asked Tommy to give this to you at Christmas because it's his favorite. I feel like Christmas is a favorite for all of the Stratford boys, mine included. They turn into little kids again this time of year and I think a lot of that is because Mama made it come to life. Can I blame them for loving it? Absolutely not. It's magical. Snow or no snow, depending on where the two of you are living, he will make it magical every single year. Wonderful things happen at Christmas, Mrs. Stratford.

In the short time Brian and I were together, I noticed Christmas was increasingly the topic of conversation once October hit. For them, it was like Halloween and Thanksgiving didn't exist. Those were merely days to take a break from planning for Christmas. I didn't get to spend Britton's first Christmas with them, but I imagine how wonderful it must have been for Kathryn to spend it with her first grandchild. I have to believe having him there made it fun all over again. Living in Tennessee, it's not very often we had snow, but my first, and last, Christmas with them, Kathryn decorated the house as though Mother Nature created a blizzard inside those four walls. I think she missed New York winters despite all the years they'd been in the south.

The year I was pregnant with Britton, Kathryn began pulling out all of her decorations right before Halloween. The boys said she was getting ready for the holiday way too soon, earlier than she had in the past, but, if I'm being honest with you, I think it's because she knew I wouldn't be there the following year. Kathryn had a way of knowing things. At that point I hadn't told Tommy I was sick. He just knew something was wrong. I waited for the conversation about my cancer coming back until after I left. You wouldn't even be getting a letter today if it wasn't for Tommy's persistence about staying in contact with me. He sent me pictures from Britt's first Christmas after I left. I wish I had been there, if for no other reason than the family. The Stratfords make every day extraordinary, and on Christmas it is just ... it's so much more.

I sent Tommy back to Tennessee with one of the pictures I took of him from the Christmas I spent with them. If he didn't take it out, it should be in the big envelope. I want you to have it. The look on Tommy's face? I hope he is always filled with that much joy — not just at Christmas. The world deserves his smile. If I know Tommy the way I think I do, you make him smile that way and I am so sorry I will never have the chance to meet the girl who makes his world spin. I feel like anyone who has the ability to come in and create an eternal sunshine for him would have been a wonderful person to be friends with. I wish you both nothing but years of bliss and love and happiness. And, God willing, lots of babies. That man was born to be a daddy.

All my love,
Emily

Chapter 33

Tommy
Britton: Age 16

"So, do you think he's going to mess up the three-point turn?"

Brian hangs his head but offers a good-natured laugh as we walk toward the Methodist church on the corner and sit on the steps. At least we have somewhere to sit near the test site. "You think he's going to be just like me in that respect?"

When Bri went for his road test, he was so nervous he'd screw up and fail — the guy who never failed at anything — that he turned right when told to turn left. He ended up on a narrow, dead end street and had to complete a five-point turn just to keep Mama's car on the road.

"Nah," he says, clasping his hands together between his knees. He looks across the street, but I don't think he's seeing the houses there. He's somewhere else. "He's practiced a lot. He'll pass without a problem."

We sit in silence, a few minutes passing us by, before he says, "You know Em left a letter for this, too?" He's had trouble with each new letter Britt has opened over the years. It's a reminder of the things he didn't know about her. He smiles sadly. "I didn't give her enough credit. All these years and I'm still trying to figure out how to make all the anger I felt go away. It's not enough to say I'm sorry, because who do I say it to?"

"Brian, you can't do that to yourself—"

"But I can."

"No, really, you can't. She knew you were going to be angry. She made sure you were. But look how far you've come? For Christ's sake, you and Stella named your daughter after her. Emily knows you're sorry. She knows."

My niece, Emiliana — Emmy for short — was born shortly after Brian and Stella were married. Britt wanted her to have a special name and the name fits her perfectly.

Brian takes a deep breath but before he can attempt to argue with me, Britt pulls up to the stop sign across the street. We watch him shake the examiner's hand. Despite the serious expression on his face, he's teeming with excitement when he gets out of the car and walks toward us.

He hands the keys to Brian without a word and we both look at him curiously.

"You didn't pass?" Brian questions.

Britt smiles. "No, I passed."

I laugh at the confusion.

"Then why are you giving me the keys?"

"Because I figured you would want to drive home."

"No way. You can drive us. Then you can go get groceries," Brian says. "And your sisters need to go to softball practice. Emmy's is at the high school, Katie's is at the middle school."

Britt offers silence in response to the list of new responsibilities. His brows knit together, but he nods his head.

"Okay, but what about work? I'm supposed to be there at four," he says.

This kid ... he is his father through and through.

"I can handle closing with Greg tonight," Brian says. "You're probably going to want a few hours of freedom since you can't be out driving past nine."

The three of us begin walking to the car. I'm a few steps behind them when I see Brian apprehensively pull an envelope from his back pocket. I can't hear what he says to Britt, but I see him flounder for words. Britton takes the paper in his hands, staring at the familiar penmanship. He pulls his father into a tight hug before going to the driver's side and climbing in.

Dear Britton,

I'm sure Dad has already gone over all the rules with you and your mom has probably given you plenty of advice on how to be safe while driving, but I just want to put my two cents in there, too.

Emily's Rules for Driving

1. Don't get cocky. If you're the first of your friends to get your driver's license, please don't show off. It's a privilege to pass that road test and be allowed to drive your parent's car on the actual road instead of just down some farmer's dirt lane between fields. Trust me on this.

2. I repeat, don't get cocky ... this is in case you're the last of your friends to get your license. Chances are, at least one of them has acted foolish and you know better than to push the envelope. Don't take the chance of losing the privilege by staying out too late (because extra chores are doable) or drag racing (because it's illegal). It's not worth taking those chances just to impress your friends.

3. ALWAYS wear your seatbelt. There are no exceptions.

4. You have a cell phone? Wonderful. They are great to have in emergencies. Do not use it while you're driving. Is social media still a thing? No posting while the car is moving. A text message or phone call is not worth your life. Pull over if you need to answer, or let it go to voicemail. (Unless you have an earpiece, in which case, the phone call thing may not apply so much. Just be careful talking while driving.)

5. Make sure you have a First Aid kit. You'll never know when you might need it.

6. Even if you live somewhere warm, keep a spare blanket with you. Buy a snowbrush, too, just in case. Weather is weird.

7. Shotgun chooses the music. This is law.

8. Keep spare cash or change in the console. You might come across someone in need of a hot cup of coffee or a bowl of soup. If you have the means, be sure to pay it forward. Blessings come back in droves.

9. Always remember I love you and want to keep you safe. I'll kick you right on out of heaven if I see you up there before you're supposed to arrive.

For what it's worth, some of these things are pieces of advice my own father gave me around the time I started driving, which even now seems like was a million years ago. But, it was advice I found useful time and again, especially number 8.

You're practically a grown up now. The piece of plastic that gives you the right to drive is so much more than just your identification, though. Someday you'll have the chance to choose to be an organ donor (and it's a huge decision to make, so make it wisely), you'll use it to get into a bar to have your first legal drink (and you're going to be sure to have a designated, sober driver with you, right?), and you'll show it to the police officer when you get your first speeding ticket (because we both know it's probably going to happen). Don't misplace it. Don't let someone else who kind of looks like you borrow it. Don't abuse it, because it can be taken away.

Love,
Emily

~*~*~*~

I bolt upright when my phone rings. I'm not used to middle of the night phone calls and panic when I see Britt's name on the screen. The kid literally just got his license. This can't be good.

"Britt? What's wrong?" I say as soon as the call connects.

"Nothing. I swear. I've been home all night, haven't been in a car accident, and I wasn't arrested," he says. I hear him start laughing on the other end, but my heart is still racing.

I mutter, "Thank God," under my breath and lay back down, rubbing the sleep from my eyes.

"If you're not in trouble, what's with the two in the morning wake-up call?"

Jacey rolls over and places her hand on my chest. I check to be sure she's still sleeping before carefully slipping out from under her arm and down to the kitchen. I'm grabbing the milk from the fridge when Britt finally says, "Should I write back?"

"Like when you were little?"

"When I was little?" he questions, confirming my suspicion that he doesn't remember.

I pour a glass of milk and place the jug back in the fridge before answering him.

"When you were, I don't know, probably four or five years old, you would draw pictures or spend hours coloring. They weren't nearly as good as what you draw these days, but they were pretty amazing considering you were just a little guy."

I'm trying to find words and I can't. I kept the pictures, though. He only drew them when Mama and I were with him while Brian was working. He stopped drawing them after Brian and Stella got together.

"You used to draw pictures of your mom. Not all the time," I tell him, "but, every once in a while, you'd sit down and draw her. Grandma Kathryn and I figured out long before your dad knew that you knew Emily had passed away."

Memories I didn't realize I needed to dredge up come flooding back as I think about how connected this kid was to a mother he never knew.

"After each picture you finished, you would ask if I would send it to 'the angel.' You used to say, 'the angel came to see me.' And, you know, we just didn't question it," I say.

"I remember that," he says. "She stopped coming after Mom and Dad got married though."

"Because she knew you were in good hands. The most important thing to Emily was making sure you were safe and happy," I say. "And you are. So, if part of your happiness as a young man means responding to the letters from Emily, then I think you should do it."

"I love you, Uncle Tommy," he says.

He's a tough kid, but when it comes to the women in the family and his connection with them, he's gooey. I like him that way.

"Love you, too."

Dear Emily,

I passed my road test today. Dad gave me your letter and ... thank you. I let Mom read it when I was done and she laughed. I'm pretty sure you thought of some rules she hadn't, though most were close to identical. I think you would have liked her. My mom is pretty amazing.

Dad acted strange when he gave me this one. I'm not sure what was going through his mind, but each time he gives me a new letter from you he seems a little overwhelmed. I tried asking him about it once and instead of answering me, he grabbed me and bearhugged me half to death. He does a good job, I just wonder sometimes if he wishes you were still here, too. Maybe some of this would be easier for him.

Usually when Dad gives me one of your letters, I put it in my dresser with the rest of them and don't share them. This time I didn't hide it away. I actually left it under a mug next to the coffee maker. Mom saw it and gave me a look. I told her I wanted Dad to read this one, too. He found it when he came in from the coffeehouse tonight. He said to me, "I didn't give her enough credit." I don't think any of us have.

You've been gone fourteen years and he still feels guilty for not knowing what was going on. He's told me time after time he wishes he had done better but, between you and me, it is what it is. You've given me so many opportunities to know you through your letters that I don't feel like I missed out. Plus, Grandma Long calls me every week. She fills in the gaps. Without Uncle Tommy, I wouldn't have even had a relationship with her at all. Without Tommy, I wouldn't have these bits and pieces of you, either. I know you're not here, physically, but you're still here. Somewhere.

Love,
Britt

P.S.: Number 8 is my favorite.

Chapter 34

Tommy
Britton: Age 18

I see the envelope in Brian's suit pocket as he unbuttons the jacket. He catches my eye and pats his chest where the letter is hidden beneath the fabric and smiles at me.

"She thought of everything," he says. "There's one more at the house that I can't give him until it's time."

I smirk. I know. He's going to tell me anyway.

"It's for when he finds his one," he says close to my ear. "I hope I have more than a couple years to prepare myself for giving that one to him. I'm hoping he'll focus on college first."

Britt has busted his ass to complete courses outside the high school curriculum, to the point he's only a few credits shy of an associate's degree already. "He's driven, Bri. I don't think you need to worry about where his focus is. Just hold onto that letter for when it's needed."

As the graduating class files in, I'm amazed at how far we've all come. When Emily showed up at Brian's apartment with that first picture of Britt, I never in my wildest dreams could have imagined how much of an impact he would have on our lives. Somewhere along the line, Britt became the glue that held us all together. While Mama and Dad always taught us about the importance of family, I sometimes think it took Emily leaving Britt for us all to truly appreciate one another and what we had right in front of us.

Britt has given me credit for the opportunity to know his mother and grandmother, but I was just the messenger.

"Please welcome this year's valedictorian, Britton Stratford," the superintendent says.

Britt's name booms through the auditorium and is met with cheers and whistles. He's the first out of the kids to graduate. He's setting the bar high for his sisters and cousins, but he's also setting the best example he can for all of them.

I listen intently as he speaks to his fellow graduates, reminding them that this is just the beginning. Their best years were not high school, nor will they be college. He exudes confidence and maturity as he speaks from a place I didn't discover until I was well into adulthood.

"Before I excuse myself and find my seat back with my classmates, I just want to give you all a few words of advice from my mom. Now, not a lot of people know this, but my birth mother passed away from Leukemia when I was a toddler. I never knew her," he says to a silent room. "But I have gotten to know her over the last several years through letters she left me ... so many letters."

He didn't tell us this part of his speech. I don't even know if he knew it was part of his speech, but I see Brian and Stella beaming proudly as Britt continues.

"I want each of you tonight to leave here and know what that kind of love feels like. So, here are some driving tips that serve well also as life tips from my mom, Emily Long," he says. Clearing his throat, he begins again, "First one, don't get cocky. That's also the second one. She wanted to make sure I kept my ego in check. Thanks, Mom."

He laughs along with those of us in the audience before continuing. "Third? Always wear your seatbelt. Rule number five is a big one. Get yourself a First Aid Kit because you just never know when you're going to need one. I think we all know seven, but just to make sure we're clear ... shotgun chooses the tunes."

I watch as my nephew takes a deep breath and wipes his face. I look at Brian and Stella, Steph and Max, Caryn and Greg, and the people in the row behind us I have never met as they each try to keep themselves composed.

"And the last one I'll share is her number eight," Britt says as he stares out into the crowd as though he's looking directly at each and every one of us.

Jacey grips my hand and leans into my shoulder.

"Emily would be so proud of him," she whispers.

I couldn't agree more.

"Eight. I'm not going to paraphrase this one, though, because it's my favorite," he says. "Keep spare cash or change in the console. You might come across someone in need of a hot cup of coffee or a bowl of soup. If you have the means, be sure to pay it forward. Blessings ... blessings come back in droves."

He doesn't say anything more, just turns and walks back to his seat beside the salutatorian, a young girl who looks at him like he hung the moon. She hands him a box of tissues and then I see it.

She's his one.

Dear Britton,

Congratulations! Today you achieved the biggest accomplishment of your teen years. Graduating high school is just the first step, sweetie.

I'm sorry I've missed out on all these years with you and that I am not able to be there to watch you walk up and shake your superintendent's hand as they pass your diploma to you. I'm proud of you and whatever your accomplishments are. I'm proud of you no matter if you go to college like your daddy or if you choose to go into a vocation. If I know your dad like I think I do, you've had a lot of years of knowing that hard work pays off.

When you were a newborn, I envisioned what it would be like to sit and watch all these amazing moments you're having and the ones you're about to embark on. I would sit quietly and rock you in the middle of the night imagining you playing T-ball and soccer like your dad and Uncle Tommy. I hate that I'm missing all of this, but thankful every day that the choices I made meant you had the chance to do everything a little boy should do.

And now you're a grown man. It's kind of difficult to comprehend all the little moments I will miss, and have already missed, with you. All I ask is that as you go out into the world, you treat people with kindness. Be nice. Hold doors open for others. Help little old ladies with their groceries. Offer to walk the neighbor's dog. Hold that girl's hand during the scary parts of the movie. Just be kind while you're doing these things. I think sometimes people forget how much a kind word can mean to someone else. I've learned these things from your daddy. They were lessons I had started to forget before I met him. I forgot people could be kind just because they wanted to be.

Brian has always been one to give gentle direction. He guided others with love and, even though you were an infant when I left, I could see his parenting would be filled with the same. In the months leading up to meeting you, I watched closely as he interacted with people around us. Mostly, there was a lot of him carefully pushing Tommy closer to the path he was supposed to be on. At times their relationship was strained because of it, but never broken, and they always had each other to lean on. I pray you have a little brother or sister, or both, to help guide like your dad did with Tommy.

If you've made the decision to leave home and go to college, remember to call frequently. Texting is great, but a video chat or good old fashioned telephone call means so much more to those who love you. Relationships need to be nurtured. Like plants need sunlight and water, relationships need attention, too. Intimacy, love, mutual respect, open communication, affection … they seem like such simple things, but really, they make all the difference. Don't cut them out or you cut off the lifeline to those who care about you most of all.

I know you're just leaving high school and preparing for the next phase in life, but what if your next phase includes falling in love? I'm not there to see that happen and knowing I'll never see you as a grown up, as a married man, or as a father is scaring me a little right now.

I wish I had some idea what your plans are, or where you're going to end up. I wish I could give you the world.

Love,
Emily

Dear Emily,
You did give me the world.
I love you,
Britt

Chapter 35

Tommy
Britton: Age 25

"Are you absolutely sure?" Brian asks as we wait at the bar for our drinks.

Tonight, we're celebrating Britt's ever-growing portfolio. He just accepted a position at a graphic design company in downtown Rochester, but he's also got his hands full with the art studio Jacey helped him open a few years ago. It's a family investment. He was such an integral part of Jacelyn's studio when we first opened that he wanted to expand her reach and bring art to the inner city.

"Were you sure when you asked Mom?" he asks. He turns to look at me. "And were you positive she was it when you asked Aunt Jacey?"

I see Brian bite his lip. I shift my feet and shove my hands in my pockets. That's all the answer Britt needs, and he pats his father on the shoulder.

"If I wasn't one hundred percent certain, I would wait," he says.

There's no containing his smile.

She's his one.

I'll always think of her as the girl with the tissues.

Now I'll also get to know her as my niece.

He's had the ring picked out for months and I can't wait for my nephew to finally begin the rest of his life with Adira. She's one of the sweetest girls we've ever met and, to be absolutely honest, she seems to have been hand-picked for him.

I take a long pull on my bottle of beer as Brian reaches into his jacket.

Britt laughs. "She didn't want to miss any of it, did she?"

"I guess not," Brian says, handing the envelope to his son. "We'll give you a few minutes. Just let us know when it's time."

My brother and I walk away, but I turn back and watch as Britt carefully breaks the seal on the last envelope. Emily tried to finish all of the letters she had planned, but she didn't get past this one. I know she wanted to write one for when he becomes a dad himself, but she was so tired. I can only imagine how much it took from her to get to this one.

Britt carefully unfolds the letter, and then a smile appears.

Dear Britton,

I don't know if soulmates exist but, if they do, I pray you have found yours. Make sure she knows every day that you love her with all your heart.

Make each other smile.

Buy her flowers but send them a day or two before your anniversary so she gets to enjoy them longer.

Do the things that give her butterflies. All those little things you did when love was new? Do those throughout the course of a lifetime.

Kiss her in a way that makes her weak in the knees. Be sure to hold her up. When you need her to be the strength, she'll lift you until you can hold your own.

Love is a two-way street. It doesn't just happen — it takes work. It's 50-50, but the weight shifts. Don't be an anchor, be a flotation device. You'll need to save one another throughout time.

Arguing is normal, but don't go to bed angry. If you do, still hold her hand as you fall asleep.

Be present.

Love,
Emily

Dear Mom,

She said yes.
Her knees went weak.
I haven't stopped smiling.

I love you,
Britt

Epilogue

Britt

It's springtime in Mississippi and the moisture thickened breeze leaves my arms sticky beneath the fabric of my shirt, but my palms are sweaty for another reason. Today, I'm going to meet my mother.

Placing the envelope under my arm, I unbutton and roll up the sleeves of my dress shirt. I pull a pair of aviator sunglasses from my pocket, sliding them into place to block out the sun as I step away from the car and into the deep, emerald grass. My fire engine red Chucks leave footprints in the dew, every step an imprint on the earth, a memory that I will nurture. Cresting a small hill, the residents in this house come into view. Each row is perfectly straight, the stones lined up and uniform like soldiers standing at attention. Grandma Long gave me the directions — four rows back, third one in from the left of the dirt path — and I find her easily.

Emily Marie Long
Loving daughter and mother
Age 29

It's a simple, sleek green stone. Her birth and death dates aren't engraved in the granite, but they don't need to be. Those are dates I have burned in my memory. It's difficult to forget the day your mother died when it also is the day you received a new one.

Mom and Dad didn't know their wedding date happened to be on the anniversary of Emily's death. The story goes they originally planned to get married at the beginning of April but with Mom being pregnant with my sister, Emmy, she needed to have last minute alterations to her dress. It kicked the wedding back by about ten days, falling on April 22. No one really noticed, though, since there never were formal invites. It was a few days after their wedding before Uncle Tommy told them why the day was both a joyful and sorrowful occasion for him.

I smile at the memory of hearing the story the first time as an adult.

That's what life is. It's a collection of stories. Stories are why I'm here.

Mine needs an end. Perhaps it's more of a beginning. I'm not entirely sure at this point, but I know this is a pivotal moment.

There just isn't a letter from Emily this time.

Over the years I've become accustomed to the major events in my life being preceded or followed by my dad warily handing me a yellowed envelope with loopy script scrawled across the middle — "Britton, for when you get your license," one says while another has words jumping off the paper yelling, "Britton, for your graduation," and still another proudly proclaims, "Britton, for when you find your 'one'." That's not including all the little notes she wrote in between because she simply wanted to talk to me or the ones from when she was pregnant with me and trying to figure out her emotions. There has to be at least a hundred letters and notes in the envelope in my hand.

I knew Dad would have another letter for me the night I proposed to Adira. I wasn't prepared, though, for it to be the last one I would receive.

Kneeling in front of the stone, I remove my sunglasses. I press the tip of my index finger into the creases of the "E" before moving on to the "M," tracing each letter carefully and, when I finally get to the "Y," I lose my composure. I'm a little boy again, afraid of the dark and crying out for my dad to save me. I'm gripped by the well-known fear that I will never know her except through her words. I'll never have the chance to stand before her and tell her how much she has meant to me all these years.

I can't hug her and thank her for giving me all of her when there was so little left for her to keep for herself.

Does she hear me when I talk to her? Is she still around, somewhere in the ether?

Adira said she would come with me, but I asked her to let me do this on my own. Still, she was willing to drop everything and get on the plane with me this morning. She asked if I wanted Dad to meet me in Biloxi, and I shook my head. Instead of answering, I kissed her deeply at the security checkpoint and reminded her I would be home in a few days. I encouraged her to spend the time looking for her wedding gown. October is going to be here before we know it and we have hardly started planning.

Maybe I should have let her come. Maybe I should have had Dad join me. Maybe I shouldn't have done this on my own.

I suck back the next sob as it climbs my throat, threatening to break the solitude of this hallowed space. At twenty-five, I thought I had a good handle on how I would feel when I finally took this step.

I lied to myself. Doing this won't bring her back. Coming here doesn't make it easier.

"I wish there were more letters. I wish there was more of you to hold onto," I say between gasping breaths. I know I wasn't there when she went home, but all the same that last letter was final, and I say, "It felt like you were dying all over again."

Each new letter came with the possibility it would be the last. But still, I always looked forward to them. I expected them. Birthdays and Christmases, a little note jotted on a napkin from the wedding where she and Dad met. She wrote about Grandma Kathryn and Uncle Tommy. She left behind mementos of her childhood. There's a weathered piece of loose-leaf paper with a story she shared with me about skinning her knee when she learned to ride a bike.

She gave me all of her memories.

She filled me with life lessons.

She accentuated each of my important days; she was the exclamation point at the end of every achievement.

I don't have the energy to say more to her. I've been talking to her my entire life and here is where I lose the ability to form sentences. Finally, sitting here with her, I'm out of words.

Touching this cold stone is my closure.

My arms drape over the top of her as my tears rain down, cleaning a thin layer of dust and dirt from the smooth arch above her name, when I feel strong hands on my shoulders. I feel the relief of not being alone roll through my body as he kneels beside me.

"She loved you, Britt. You have to know that," Dad says in my ear, his voice thick with emotion. I nod my head, but I feel my heart clench in my chest and it burns. "You were the best gift she ever could have given me. She must be so proud of the man you've become."

I feel myself being pulled toward him and for the first time in a dozen years I find myself curled up in my father's lap, clinging to him as I cry out all of my goodbyes.

And when my goodbyes are gone, I feel full still.
Full of her, of life, of love.
She's given me a million gifts in the span of a hundred letters.
She's given me stories.
She's given me the world.

Also by M.L. Pennock

The *To Have* Series

To Have — Brian and Stella's story
To Hold — Stephanie and Max's story
To Cherish — Tommy and Jacelyn's story

Acknowledgments

Emily wasn't supposed to have a story.

Emily was just a secondary character I never intended to flesh out.

At the time, I needed an absent mother to explain why Brian was a single father … and then I gave her cancer. For good measure, I made sure Tommy knew she was sick and had been given the task of telling his brother. Then, the memory of her arrived in Tommy and Jacey's story. She wouldn't stop harassing me from the moment Tommy told Jacelyn about brushing Emily's hair while she was sick. She was relentless.

I'm so glad she was, because through her I've had the chance to watch Britton grow up — and let me tell you, that hasn't been easy. I was conflicted. I felt like I needed to purge this story all at once while also feeling as though holding back and only sharing a little at a time was more appropriate. As a mother, I had a hard time letting Britt become an adult. When it happened, though, he wrote the beginning of his own story as Emily's was ending.

This story wrote itself. It was meant to be a short novella. I planned for it to be in the 20,000-word range. By the time I finished, Emily's story more than doubled that. As I've told many people, she had a lot to say. In turn, I was able to continue giving Tommy Stratford a voice and then, as you've seen, Britt was able to lend his own voice. That wasn't supposed to happen either. Britt was supposed to read the letters, not respond. But then? Then I found myself writing about him calling his uncle and, well, Britt made his own decisions.

I have trouble thinking about these characters — this family — as two-dimensional when they have such vivid personalities. I hope you've felt the same way. I hope you'll continue to travel with me on this journey as I continue to discover the people living and loving in the small community I've built.

When I first told people I was writing Emily's book next, I was hoping it wasn't a major let down — Caryn and Greg still need to tell their story and there has been definite interest in hearing more from Fisher after introducing him in *To Cherish*. To skip over already present characters who have very loud voices seemed risky at the time. It's a risk I'm glad I took.

The family and friends who listened to me as I wrote each of Emily's letters and read snippets out of context only increased my need to finish this story.

Their encouragement hasn't wavered once since the beginning and I'm lucky to have them in my corner.

Mom, being the first to read this book, your comments and suggestions were exactly what I needed for a story that pertains to such a heavy topic. I'm so glad you are able to be part of this process with me. I know the subject matter hit close to home, but the lessons I learned from you helped me shape this book and tackle Emily's story with grace.

Ron, Liz, and Jen, I can't thank you enough for beta reading and editing Emily's story. I'm not sorry you cried.

To my ARC team and members of my author group, I appreciate each and every one of you for your involvement and dedication. I'm glad to have found so many kindred spirits.

Heather, thank you for the time you put into this project and your enthusiasm when it came to making Emily's cover perfect. I am so fortunate to be able to work with you and blessed to call you a friend.

Anyone who knows me, knows of my deep love for coffee. It's creative fuel when drinking wine too early in the day is frowned upon. In the few short years since I began this trek through the indie publishing world, there's one person who has consistently made sure I have my fill of caffeine humor — virtual pick-me-ups, if you will. Thank you, Mrs. Smith, for all the memes, links to Facebook pages, articles, and conversation. More than those, though, I thank you for the journal assignments my senior year of high school. Without them, I don't know how many more years it would have taken me to try to write something other than crappy poetry during Parnell's chemistry and physics classes.

About the Author

M.L. Pennock is a former journalist turned author. She attended Alfred University, earning a Bachelor of Arts in English and communication studies, before going on to earn a Master of Arts in communications from SUNY College at Brockport. She lives in Central New York with her husband and three daughters.

M.L. Pennock is the author of the To Have series.

Visit facebook.com/mlpennock or mlpennock.com for more information about what she's working on next.